HOGLEG HELL

Morgan smelled something he couldn't identify. It was like the smell of a decomposed body, but it had another quality to it.

Behind him, Kinnelly smelled the odor too. "It's the damn demon!" He turned and bolted away from the light. Morgan charged after him, grabbed him from behind and spun him around.

"It's just a smell. There's not a damn thing to worry about."

Kinnelly's face was a mask of terror. "I can see something back there. Look!" Before Morgan could stop him, Kinnelly pulled a six-inch hunting knife from his belt and threw it down the dark tunnel.

The next second Morgan heard the knife hit the rocks of the tunnel. Suddenly sparks flew and the far end of the rocky tube exploded with a roar of deadly flames....

Also in the *Buckskin* Series:

BUCKSKIN #36

HOGLEG HELL

KIT DALTON

LEISURE BOOKS NEW YORK CITY

A LEISURE BOOK®

March 2006

Published by

Dorchester Publishing Co., Inc.
200 Madison Avenue
New York, NY 10016

ISBN 0-8439-3476-X

Visit us on the web at www.dorchesterpub.com.

HOGLEG HELL

Chapter One

Lee Buckskin Morgan felt like a kid being called in front of the headmaster in some strict English prep school. No good reason he should feel that way. He had met important people before. This one would be no different. Still, he had the feeling again. So Mrs. Wheeler was a legend in San Francisco. So what? He'd talked to legends before.

A formally dressed ancient black butler met Morgan at the door of what looked to him like a 20-room hilltop mansion. The butler led Morgan along a hall lined with original oil landscape paintings bursting with reds and yellows, soft greens and masses of multicolored flowers in a dozen different framed gardens.

Then the liveried butler ushered him down another hall with eighteenth century portraits marching along in lockstep, each with sad eyes, burnt umber clothing and ultramarine backgrounds. They stopped at a door of polished teak with a gold doorknob. The black man opened the panel and motioned Morgan inside.

Morgan stepped through the doorway into a cool library lined with hundreds of shelved books and a wide table festooned with fancy magazines. At first it was so dark he couldn't see anyone; then slowly his eyes adjusted to the light and he saw an elderly woman seated in a cherry-wood chair near the window.

She was Wilma Vandercovering Wheeler. She pulled back curtains and let more light into the room. Through the large window he saw a magnificent view of San Francisco Bay.

"Whatever in the world happened to common courtesy?" the old voice crackled, edged with impatience and a touch of anger.

"Ma'am?" Lee Morgan asked.

"Young man, don't try to bluff me. I sent you a letter a full two weeks ago asking you to see me on a most urgent matter." She frowned, pinching her lined and pallid face into ever deepening furrows. "You're just like your father. I used to know him, many years ago. Buckskin Frank Leslie. I hear you're twice as ornery as he was, just as hard to kill and will take on almost any job as long as it's fairly honest and pays well. That true?"

"You knew my father?"

"Yes, knew him well. He didn't spend all of his time up there in Idaho on that moth-eaten, scurvy horse ranch he called the Spade Bit. Fact is he did some work for me now and then. No matter. What I want to do is get a look at you. Step over here by the window where my old eyes can get a better reading on this Lee Buckskin Morgan."

He moved closer to the window. Today he had fancied up and wore his one good suit, an expensive navy blue wool with a white shirt and soft blue silk tie. His black town shoes had a sheen on them he could shave in. His blondish brown, freshly cut hair was neatly combed.

He'd been told this grand dame of San Francisco was 83, owned half of the town, and didn't mind letting people know it.

The old woman saw a man who stood six feet tall and weighed a compact 185 pounds of tough muscle. He was clean shaven, had brown eyes and a strong mouth. He carried in his hand his favorite brown, low-crowned Stetson with a headband of black crowded with red painted diamonds.

She nodded after a close scrutiny. "Yep, I can see it. You've got his chin and his nose. Course, Frank was much better looking than you are. Still I hear you have the girls all atwitter. I can see a lot of Frank in you, boy. Oh, yes, I remember your Pa. I knew him well. Too well sometimes.

"Can you draw that tied-down hogleg like Frank could? Pretend the door is a gunman. Draw on him, now!" She barked the last word.

Morgan frowned down at her. "Ma'am, usually I don't draw down on a door, unless I'm aiming to shoot."

"Morgan don't go yellow on me, damn it. Draw!" she stamped one black high-buttoned shoe for emphasis.

Morgan's right hand rested near his right leg. He jerked his hand upward until his palm hit the grip of the .45 Peacemaker. The heavy weapon rose out of its leather and his finger clawed for the trigger guard. By the time the muzzle of the barrel cleared leather, he had his finger on the trigger, had cocked the hammer with his thumb and pushed the weapon forward in an aim-and-shoot motion. Morgan figured the draw took perhaps a tenth of a second.

"Oh, yes," Mrs. Wheeler said. "You just might be faster than Frank was. Hard to compare so many years apart." She watched him.

Morgan was an expert with every kind of weapon, handgun, rifle, knife, rope and even the black-snake whip. He could also defend himself with bare knuckles and some Oriental-style kicks and hand thrusts. He could track like an Indian and move through brush and trees without making a sound.

"Morgan, you broke as usual? I've done some checking on you. Your pa always was so broke he'd take on impossible jobs."

Morgan coughed. "Well, Mrs. Wheeler, I'm not exactly bulging my bank account with cash money."

"You don't even have a bank account. I studied up on you these past two weeks I've been waiting."

Morgan chuckled. "No bank account at the moment. Have had one in the past. It always seemed to come up empty, somehow."

"You're sounding more like Frank Leslie all the damn time. How did you get my message?"

"I have a friend here in town who collects mail for me when I'm away. I just came back from Colorado. Got in yesterday and raced right over here. I've taken to San Francisco. It's a fine town."

"It's a damn big city by now. An overrated hell-hole, where men are shanghaied for the ships, women turned into whores, and new silver and gold millionaires seduce each other's wives. A terrible place." She sighed. "But, damn it, I'm stuck here. Have been for almost sixty years. Outlived my husband, but you're not interested in all that."

She squinted at him. "I just hope you're not a damn Democrat. The President is about to finish his term in the White House. Don't know who we'll run who's as good as Rutherford Hayes. I like his vice president, William A. Wheeler, but he's not presidential material. He's got a hell of a good last name though, same as mine." She screeched with laughter for a moment.

Morgan saw that she wore no spectacles and that her small body was thin, her movements slow.

"You ready to go to work?" she asked.

"Maybe, after you tell me what the job is, where I have to go, what I have to do and . . . how much I get paid."

Wilma Wheeler threw back her head and laughed. He was surprised how full and deep her laugh came. She wiped her eyes with a small linen handkerchief she took from the cuff of her sleeve and then replaced it.

"Where? You go to Hangtown, up from Sacramento a ways. Gold mining country in the mountains. You find my granddaughter, Alexis Wheeler, and bring her back to me. Also want you to catch a jasper named Julio. Arrested him for kidnapping my granddaughter and bring him back for trial. Then there's one other small matter."

She stopped and peered at him. "For goodness sakes, Morgan, sit. Sit down somewhere and stop looming over me like some giant buzzard waiting for me to croak."

Morgan smiled and sat in a chair near the window. He watched her with increased interest.

"The other small matter?" he prompted.

"Yes. I have a mine in the mother lode. The Lady Luck. A good mine, produces well, or used to. Six months ago, they dug into what I figure is an old Indian burial cave. Must have been a cave that got blocked from the outside by a landslide. Six months ago our men tunneled into it from inside the mountain.

"Now my mine is shut down. The workers claim that the digging set free a demon named Alkazack, and that he's been a deadly menace ever since. Them ninnies say this demon has caused the deaths of four miners and even reversed the flow of water in one of the tunnels. The men say he snuffed out the miners' lamps and candles on one whole level, leaving them in darkness.

"All of the workers in the tunnel had to grope their way out in total darkness.

"As a result of these ridiculous rumors and story-telling, my mine has been shut down for over six months. My business manager say I'm losing twenty thousand dollars a month on the shut down mine.

"That's the rest of your job, to find and kill this damn demon, or whatever he is. Destroy the rumors and wild stories and get the mine back in operation."

Morgan grinned and stood. He walked around the room and then came back and sat down. "You believe this is a demon, straight out of the Bible records?"

Mrs. Wheeler fidgeted in her chair. She looked out the window, then back. "As a good Christian woman, it makes it hard not to. Bible says that God threw out the bad angels, including this Alkazack. You know about black and white, hot and cold, up and down. You believe in one, then you got to believe in the other. Can't be no up without a down. Can't be no God without a Devil, and his little friend, Alkazack.

"What about you, Morgan? You believe in devils and demons?"

"Just ain't met one face to face." He grinned. "Course I ain't met God face to face neither."

Morgan stared out at the San Francisco Bay and the tall ships moving in and out. "Mrs. Wheeler, you don't ask for much. Why haven't you hired one of the detective agencies here in San Francisco to do the job?"

"I wanted you."

"But I wasn't your first choice, was I?"

The old woman took a long breath, then shook her head. "No, I talked with detectives here in town. They wouldn't take the job."

"Why? They must have given you some reason they turned down what must be a high-priced assignment."

The small woman leaned forward. She grasped a heavy headed cane and scowled at him.

"Of course they gave me a reason. Why should I tell you?"

"If they didn't want this job, maybe I don't want it for the same reason. Why wouldn't they take the assignment?"

"Morgan, I want justice in this case. I also want revenge. That Julio has stolen my companion, my little girl, the best reason for me to keep on living. I raised Alexis since she was four when her parents were killed in a fire. She's my only living relative."

"I understand. Why didn't the other detectives take the job?"

Mrs. Wheeler lifted a long thin cigar from a tray on a nearby table and struck a match. She lit the brown tobacco, inhaled a long pull of the smoke and blew it out. A hacking cough followed.

"Yes, yes, I know. Smoking is bad for my throat, but at my age what have I got to lose? I've already outlived two of my doctors."

She pulled on the cigar again. "The people in Hangtown tell us that the demon has bragged that he will shut down every mine in the area. Then he'll take Alexis as his bride."

Morgan saw the old woman breathe deeply twice, then sniffle and shake her head. She blinked her eyes as they filled with tears that soon spilled down wrinkled cheeks.

"Save my baby girl, Lee Buckskin Morgan. I'll pay you ten thousand dollars if you can save her and seal up that demon."

Morgan was caught off guard by her pleading and her tears. She was a tiger around San Francisco's social set. She supported more charities than he had heard of and had a hand in picking the last mayor.

He stalled. "Mrs. Wheeler, I don't know what to say. I've never tangled with a real demon before. The only ones I've battled turned out to be all too human. Is there a chance that someone is simply trying to scare you out of the mine so he can buy it cheap?"

"Of course. The first detective I hired told me the same thing. The second one agreed that might be the problem. The first man I sent to Hangtown came back two weeks later and threw my advance money at my feet and said never to contact him again."

Morgan frowned. Getting more and more interesting. "What about the second detective?"

"We don't know. He was there a week, went into the mine one day and no one has seen nor heard of him since."

Morgan pushed his feet out and leaned comfortably against the back of the chair. "Do you mind if I smoke?" She shook her head. He pulled out one of his long black cheroots, bit off the end, fired it with a match and with the first smoke blew a perfect ring at the ceiling. Then he fixed his glance on the small woman.

"This story is starting to get interesting, Mrs. Wheeler. One killed and one scared off. Do you have anything written down about the mine, the town, your granddaughter and this demon?"

The small woman rose with more agility than he thought possible, marched to a small desk at the far side of the room and came back with an envelope. She wore a soft gray dress with blue lace over it. The costume covered her from her corded neck to her wrists and swept the floor. A delicate cameo broach showed at her throat. He figured she stood no taller than four foot ten inches.

She handed him a brown envelope. "It's all there. Everything I know about it. Now, will you take the job?"

"How many have turned it down?"

Her blue eyes sparked fire. "You really want an honest answer?"

"Absolutely."

"Eight different detective agencies told me no. Seven here in town and another one from Los Angeles. Everyone refused the job. Even a one-man agency that began a month before. No one will take the case."

Morgan puffed on the cigar and grinned. "Just my cup of tea, Mrs. Wheeler. The kind of a challenge that I like. Looks like you have three jobs here. I'll charge you five thousand dollars for each one. I get rid of the demon or eliminate the threat of the demon so he's no problem. I rescue your granddaughter from Julio. I bring Julio to justice for kidnapping Alexis, if that's a legal charge."

"Done! And done again, to quote the Bard," the small woman whispered. She stepped forward and shook Morgan's hand vigorously. "I have a bank draft for five thousand dollars here as an advance. All I need to do is write your name on it. I'll pay your expenses up to twenty dollars a day."

She stood there a moment watching him. "There's more of Frank Leslie in you than I expected. Oh, I've heard of your exploits and shenanigans around Idaho, Washington, Oregon and the southwest. Shades of the first Buckskin. Now I can see that most of the stories must be true. I think you just might find my little girl after all."

She looked at a chiming clock on the wall. "Oh, my, I'm nearly late. I have a bridge tournament. I'm in the final set of four tables. I might even win this thing if my partner can stay awake."

"I can find my way out," Morgan said.

"Ridiculous, that's why I hire help."

The moment Morgan stepped out the library door, the same liveried black man who had shown him in led him to the front door. With that five thousand dollar check in his hand, Morgan didn't even notice the fine art on the walls.

Outside, Morgan grinned as he thought about the check. Now he'd open a bank account and keep enough cash to cover his expenses. First he wanted to do some research on demons at the public library.

It took him an hour to find what he wanted. There it was in black and white type. Alkazack was the fifth most imporant archangel until he was thrown out of heaven with the Devil himself. The Devil and 50 of the angels who sided with him—including Alkazack—were pitched into hell.

Morgan read it again, then closed the book and headed for his bank and then his hotel. He'd be on the train the next morning for Sacramento, then catch a stage into the mountains to Hangtown.

Morgan hadn't been there for some time. He wondered if it had changed much. Then he grinned. Of course it had changed—there was a wild, frightening, evil demon running amuck in the town. Morgan snorted and checked to be sure his Peacemaker was firmly in leather. He'd never seen a demon yet that could stand up to a pair of well-placed .45 rounds.

Was Alkazack the same kind of human "demon" he'd clouted before, or was he one with some real demonic powers? Morgan would believe the supernatural when this "demon" proved it.

Morgan picked up his key at the hotel desk and saw someone staring at him. The man came over quickly.

"Mr. Morgan, Buckskin Morgan?"

"Yes."

"I know Mrs. Wheeler has talked to you about the Lady Luck mine. Please don't go up there. I did and I nearly died. I don't think I'll ever be the same again. This Alkazack is a real demon. Even when I'm here, a hundred miles away, he still haunts me. If you want to keep your sanity, Mr. Morgan, refuse to have anything to do with the Lady Luck mine or that demon, Alkazack!"

Chapter Two

Lee Buckskin Morgan stepped off the stagecoach from Sacramento, adjusted his spine, which had been shaken, rattled and battered half into the next county, and picked up his carpet bag. His .45 hung comfortably on his right hip and he shouldered the new Spencer carbine and headed for the hotel.

He saw two, chose the larger hostelry and registered. The woman behind the desk watched him as he signed his name. She read it as he turned the book around.

"Well, Mr. Morgan, we're glad to have you staying at the White Quartz Hotel. Do you have any choice where you'd like to have your room?"

Morgan caught a subtle flirting in the woman's tone. He smiled. She was tall, with soft brown hair, a fine smile and dimples in both cheeks. She looked slender but the desk shielded most of her. Her breasts showed large and bold behind the white blouse, which had two open buttons at the top so he could almost, but not quite, see the promise of cleavage.

"Well Miss . . ." he paused.

"Oh, I'm Helen Curley. My pa owns this hotel. I'm usually around here."

"Miss Curley, I would prefer the second floor on the front so I can watch Hangtown's main thoroughfare."

"That old mud trail? It's either ankle deep in dirt or mud. I sorely miss the paving blocks they put down on some of the streets in Sacramento. Makes it all so much more civilized."

"Then you're new in town?"

"Pa and me been here for two years. Gold brought him. He doesn't dig it. He says he coins it from them who want to dig and who do dig and the owners who reap the profits."

"Miss Curley, you might know a man I'm here to meet. He goes by the name of Julio."

The girl grinned and the start of a blush swept up from her chest and tinged her neck.

"Yes, I've heard of him. I don't know where he lives, but I've heard he has an office of sorts down beyond the General Store."

"Thank you. What's my room number?"

"Oh, I'm sorry, I wasn't paying attention to business. Pa would have a fit." She made some notes on a chart and handed him a key. "You're in Room 212, that's front center. I hope it's all right. If you need anything, you just let me know."

Helen Curley smiled softly as she said it and she let her fingers stroke across his hand as she gave him the long thin key for the door.

Morgan grinned. "Miss Curley, I'll certainly remember that."

She smiled. "Welcome to Hangtown."

Morgan had just unpacked his few belongings, and cleaned his six-gun after the dusty ride into town, when a knock sounded on the door. He frowned, drew his Colt and went to the wall beside the doorknob.

"Yes, who is it?" he called.

There was no answer. The knock came again, not hard, more tentative. Morgan reached over and unlocked the door, then turned the knob and swung it open a foot.

Helen Curley stood there looking back down the hall. She had two towels over her arm.

"Mr. Morgan. I wondered if you might need some towels. You know, like for a bath or something."

She looked both ways in the hall again. No one was there. She grinned, stepped inside his room and deftly shut the door with her foot.

"Sorry, the towels were the only excuse I could think of to come up to your room."

Morgan smiled. "You really didn't need an excuse."

She stepped close to him, reached up and caught his face with her hands and kissed his lips. Her mouth burned against his and she gave a little sigh as she broke away.

"Oh, my! Now that was just as fine as I figured it would be. A girl never knows just thinking about it. That was so fine."

She picked up one of his hands and put it on her full breasts.

"Oh, glory, Lee Morgan, I love your hand there. That is just ever so good. Damn, I don't have the time to play right now, but I wanted you to know that I will come back when we both can spend a night or two together."

"Sounds like a good idea," Morgan said. His hand caressed her breasts through the fabric. Then

he unbuttoned the fasteners of her white blouse
and spread back the sides. She wore no camisole
and her full, naked breasts surged out. She smiled
at him.

Morgan bent and kissed the orbs, licked her
hard throbbing nipples, and then straightened and
kissed her lips hard, pulling her breasts against
his chest. When it ended, he kissed her nose, then
buttoned her white blouse to the top.

"Keep those beauties safe for me," he said, his
voice husky from the desire billowing in him.

She nodded, reached down and rubbed his
crotch, which had developed a long hard lump.

"Yes, yes. I'll be back tonight to have a long session with this guy down here. About eight?"

Morgan nodded. She opened the door a crack,
then closed it softly. "Company out there," she
said. She waited a moment, then pushed the door
outward and looked again. This time she nodded,
slipped through the space and closed his door.

The two white towels lay on the floor where
Helen Curley had dropped them when she kissed
him. Morgan grinned, picked up the towels and
put them on the dresser, and then went to the window and looked down on the dusty, rutted road-
way that had become the main street of Hangtown,
California.

Five minutes later he walked past the Hangtown
General Store. Morgan wore his working clothes,
fringed buckskin pants and a fringed shirt of the
same material. The light tan contrasted with the
darker hat he wore. He had seen no one else in
town with buckskins. His holster snugged tight
against his leg, tied down with a leather thong.

Morgan stared at the building just past the General Store. It had two doors. One side stood for-
lornly empty, with display cases at odd angles and

no stock of any kind. On the other side the window was covered with blinds. It had a fresh coat of paint on the door and entryway. Over the door hung a sign: "Mountain Mining," the black letters said. Worth a try. Morgan pushed the door open and inside found a small office with two desks, one of the newfangled typewriters, and a small dark man working over a desk half filled with papers. He glanced up.

"Yes?"

"Just got into town. I hear you're hiring."

The man·frowned, then shook his head. "You must have the wrong firm. We're just getting into operation. We don't even own a mine yet, but hope to soon."

Morgan laughed. "No, not that kind of hiring." Morgan dropped his hand and in a fraction of a second drew his six-gun and aimed it at a coal oil lamp on the man's desk.

"This kind of hiring."

The man lifted his brows. He was darker than most white men, but Morgan couldn't peg him as Mexican, part Indian, or Italian. He wasn't dark enough to be black. The man stood slowly.

"Yes, I see you can use your hogleg. Please put it away. I'm not at ease around weapons. Right now I have no need of security around the office; a mine will be different. But that's in the near future. We can use a man who is good with his weapon. If you can leave me your name and where I can contact you, I might have something in a week. Things should come to a head in that time and I'll know for sure about the mine."

"I can do that. I go by Josh, just the one name. I'm at the White Quartz Hotel. Leave a note in my box." Morgan hesitated. "I do have the right place. They said your name was Julio."

The man's expression didn't change. "The name is Julio, but that's not me. He owns the company. We're not ready to do any business just yet. I'll be in touch with you. Oh, the job pays twenty dollars a week."

Morgan nodded. "Sounds fair. I'll stay in touch." He turned and walked out of the office and up the street past the General Store to a small restaurant he had seen on the way down. So, he had met a man who worked for Julio. This one didn't look like much of a threat. He wondered where Julio was and how he could arrange to meet the man.

Morgan paused in front of the eatery. The small cafe had red and white checkered tablecloths. That always attracted him. He opened the door and went in, remembering he hadn't had anything to eat since breakfast and it was now after two in the afternoon.

Morgan ate a bowl of chili, a big roast beef sandwich and two cups of coffee. He had worked out a schedule of sorts. First he'd find the girl and keep her safe; then he'd take care of Julio, and last he'd go after the demon in the mine, if there really was one. He still favored the idea that some smart operator had done some fancy trickery and spooked half the town. These workers must be worse than a one-eyed raw-boned horse shying away from shadows.

Those were his first thoughts on how to work this case. Just to get oriented, he wanted to take a look at the Lady Luck mine and see if he could get a sense of what was going on. He had plenty of time before eight tonight.

Morgan grinned, remembering the girl's big breasts. Hell, he couldn't work all the time. A man had to get a little loving now and then.

After the meal, he asked directions to the Lady Luck mine. Two men refused to tell him, the third rolled his eyes.

"You really want to go up there?"

"Why I asked you," Morgan snapped.

"Hell, no skin off my nose. Might be off yours. Head on out the main road north for quarter of a mile. Turn left at the wagon track that leads back up the small valley there. There's a dead pine tree snag there at the turnoff. The mine is about half a mile north of the fork in the road."

Morgan thanked the man and moved in that direction. Six doors from the end of the business section of Hangtown he saw a storefront with a painted sign in the window. It said, "El Dorado County Sheriff, Hangtown Substation."

Morgan turned in at the sign and pushed open the door. A narrow counter ran across the front of the 20-foot-wide room. Behind it sat a deputy. A rack of three rifles and three shotguns centered on the far wall. The lawman looked up.

"You the deputy hereabouts?" Morgan asked.

"Feared so. You got trouble?" The man looked competent enough. He stood and had a six-gun on his hip in well-worn leather. The deputy came forward to the counter and leaned on it.

"Name's Deputy Vaughn Thurston." He held out his hand.

Morgan shook it and nodded. "Good to meet you, Deputy. I'm Lee Morgan up here on a small job. I might have need of your legal services sometime later on. I'm working for Mrs. Wilma Wheeler."

The deputy rubbed his jaw a minute. "Oh, yeah, Wheeler, the old gal who owns the Lady Luck mine. Too bad."

"You know anything about this demon story?"

The deputy shook his head. "Not first hand. Know some men who say it's a damn demon sure as all hell. Strange things happened in that mine for three days running, and after that, not a single man would go back underground."

"Strange things, Deputy? Like what?"

"Lamps blowing out for no reason, timbers falling. The bucket taking the men back up to the top of the main shaft damn near broke once. Hanging by only a few strands of cable. Spooky damn things. Won't catch me down in that dig. No sir. If'n there's a body down there, reckon I'd let them bring it out before I investigated."

"Usually you're not afraid to go down into the mines?"

"Hell, no, a gold mine is just a big hole in the ground. But not the Lady Luck. She's got something else. Some say it's a demon straight from hell. Some say other things. Me, I never seen me a demon before, but then I never seen me no damned angel either."

Morgan chuckled. "Sounds a mite like me. Part of my job is to get the mine opened and running again. Wanted to let you know I'm in town. I don't look for trouble, but sometimes it finds me."

He paused and waved, then stopped. "Oh, what do you know about a man called Julio?"

The deputy shook his head. "He ain't been in no trouble, so I don't recollect the name."

Morgan thanked the deputy and left the small office. It must be a one-man law operation. Did that mean that Hangtown had a local marshal or a police force, too? He'd have to find out. He doubted it.

It took him a half hour to walk up to the Lady Luck mine. A single guard sat in a small shack 100 yards from the tunnel entrance. The whole operation was silent and empty. Two buildings near the entrance of the mine tunnel were closed and, he figured, locked. Only a small whirlwind angled across the empty mine property, kicking up dust and parts of a tumbleweed.

A dust devil. Morgan grinned, thinking about the appropriateness of the term. The old guard stared at Morgan out of the open door.

"Son, what the blazes you doing up here?"

"Looking around. Anything happening?"

"Not so you could notice."

"No demon roaring out the tunnel mouth there with fire and brimstone dripping from his ugly body."

"Not a subject I talk about, let alone make jokes. Seen too much."

"What have you seen?"

"Seen twenty-seven men come out of level four in total darkness. Two of them damn near went crazy in the dark. Never heard of anything like that happening before. Damn strange and just scary as all get out."

"You haven't seen this demon, then?"

"God no! Don't aim to try. Like to be at peace the rest of my life."

"Nobody in the mine?"

"Not a blessed soul."

"Stamp mill not working?"

"Never a drop. Nobody will come that close to the tunnel where the demon is."

"Who started all these stories about the demon?"

"Hell, everybody."

"Who was on the crew that broke into the burial chamber?"

"That I know. Dart Philbun. He was lead man on that crew in level two. They had a drift going back a hundred feet near the end of tunnel two.

Followed a vein of good white quartz. Then their stone drills punched through an inch of rock into the cave. He told me he saw an oozing slimy thing break through the hole and boil out of there like steam. It collected on the roof of the tunnel and took the shape of a giant wolf with red eyes and long fangs dripping blood. The men ran out of there as fast as they could go."

"Did the thing chase them?"

The old man sucked in breath past stubs of black teeth. "Hell, they didn't say, just ran back to the shaft, climbed up the ladders to the first level and ran all the way out the main tunnel on level one to the clean, pure air and bright sunshine.

"Dart told me he was never so glad to be out of a tunnel in his life. Said some of that glob dripped on him and caused a huge burn mark he's still got. Damn burn won't heal up."

"This happened six months ago?" Morgan asked.

"Damn near."

"So why do you keep your job here?"

"Damn, somebody's got to do it. Figure I'm too old for the demon to be interested in. Sides, I got me a system. I figure this demon must be wild crazy for something to drink after being sealed up in there for God knows how many centuries. So I put a pint of whiskey just inside the closed doors on the tunnel every morning when I come to work.

"Next morning the bottle is gone, so I put down another one."

"You think this demon, Alkazack, drinks whiskey?" Morgan asked.

"Why not? Way I figure it he can change into any form or shape. Hell, you might be him testing me, all I know. If you be, I believe in you and the whiskey keeps coming."

"Why do you think he can change his form?"

"Guys said he came through that four-inch hole like steam and glop, and became a wolf on the top of the tunnel. Then he dropped down to the floor of the tunnel and snapped and snarled at them, his red eyes glowing like a true demon."

"Where could I find this Dart Philbun?"

"He's home mostly. Hates to go out of the house. He heard somewhere that if he kept a Bible and two crosses beside him at all times, he could ward off the demon."

"He lives in his own house?"

"Yep, down a block from the Masonic lodge hall. Cherry Street, I think it is. House painted white, blue trim, and picket fence in the front. Can't miss it."

Morgan thanked the man and headed back to town. He didn't look around for the demon. First real one he'd heard of who liked whiskey. He decided after he did a little more investigating he'd pay a visit to the mine at dusk when anyone inside couldn't see him. Then with two full kerosene lanterns and plenty of matches, he'd do a little investigation around the main tunnel of the Lady Luck mine.

First he wanted to talk to this Dart Philbun. The man sounded terrified.

On the way back to town he changed his mind. He remembered his master plan. First find the girl and take care of her. Where to look? He asked someone where the post office was and told in the Hangtown General Store.

Inside he saw a section next to the counter that had the words "U.S. Post Office" lettered on a one-by-six board. He walked up to the small counter and looked across it. He found a wall filled with pigeon holes, each evidently with a resident's name on it.

"Help?" a woman's voice asked from somewhere behind the wall of boxes.

"Yes, I need some information."

A woman in her forties came around the boxes. She wore man's pants, a shirt and a red bandanna around her brown hair. When she came to the window her face broke into a big grin with dancing brown eyes and a mouth full of white teeth.

"New in town, I'd say. I'm Emma, the postmistress. What do you need?"

"You're right, I'm new in town. I'm hunting a young girl, eighteen, named Alexis Wheeler. Know if she's still in town and where I can find her?"

"Yep." She stared at him but said nothing more. Her smile clung firmly in place.

"Could I have her address or where she's staying?"

"Can't do that. Against U.S. postal regulations to give out the addresses of any of our customers."

"I really need to find her. Her grandmother is concerned about her."

"Old Wilma Wheeler sent somebody to fetch her, I'd guess. Met that rich old lady once. She's a character. Smokes cigars!" Emma moved to the side and took a card out of a large file. She dropped it on the counter.

"Course now I can't give you no addresses. But if you was to see her card on the counter there, wouldn't be any way any fault of mine."

Morgan looked at the card. It had Alexis's name and an address, 310 Apple Street, Apt. B. He memorized it and grinned at the postmistress.

"Thanks, Emma. I'm glad you're holding up the high standards of the U.S. Postal Department."

"Hey, my job. You want to fill out a card, 'case you get any mail? We don't deliver. Boxes for the regulars and general delivery for the rest. But I like to know where you be 'case something important comes."

He told her his name and that he was at the hotel. She scribbled on a card and thanked him.

Outside Morgan adjusted his six-gun and headed for Apple Street. He had gone past the store and had just stepped into the alley when a six-gun deep in the gloom between the two story buildings hammered off two shots that sent Morgan diving for the edge of the next store.

Chapter Three

Morgan came up against the storefront with his six-gun in hand but he had heard heavy footsteps running down the alley and he was certain the bushwhacker was gone into the jumble of doors and piles of trash and delivery rigs along the alley. He lifted up and moved from side to side, but could see no one down the alley. Even in broad daylight he'd never find the skunk.

It wasn't hard to figure out who fired the shots. Julio must know why Morgan was in town. Who knew he was here? Only the deputy sheriff, who would have no reason to tell anyone, and the man in Julio's office Morgan had talked to just before he went out to look at the mine.

That small, dark man could have followed him, or had someone follow him. How did they catch on so quickly? The woman at the post office? Why would she tell anyone about him?

Somebody had figured out why he was in town

and seemed ready to stop him. Certainly it wasn't the demon, Alkazack, unless he learned how to shoot a six-gun. It could have been Julio because he didn't want anyone messing around out at the mine.

The latter idea held the most promise. So who would benefit by the closed mine in the event of a sale? He'd do some prospecting of his own the next day. For just a moment Morgan remembered the hot lead whizzing past his body and he wondered if he should move out of the hotel to some nice safe spot in the woods where he could hear anyone coming for 50 yards. He decided against it. He'd take his regular precautions about his hotel room.

He had been heading for Alexis's address, but now he wanted more background on the situation before he talked to her. It took him three questions of locals and then ten minutes of walking to find the offices of the *Hangtown Star*. It was a weekly newspaper that came out on Thursday. He sat in the small office a block over from the main thoroughfare, and read through the last issue. Nothing there about the demon.

He asked a man with ink smudged on his cheek and a green visor which issue he could find out about the demon out at the Lady Luck mine.

The man nodded curtly, took four papers from a drawer and gave them to Morgan.

"All right here. Appreciate it if you can read them here and leave them. Down to almost no under-counter stock on those four copies. I can't run out. You understand."

Morgan said he did and checked the front page of the earliest issue of the four papers.

LADY LUCK CLOSES
Workers Fear Demon's Wrath

The Lady Luck mine owned by Mrs. Wilma Wheeler of San Francisco has been closed by the resident manager T. J. Fox, who headed for San Francisco last Tuesday to report to Mrs. Wheeler.

Fox said that over half of the workers refused to enter the mine and that necessitated his closing it.

While Fox had no comment about the reason the miners would not go underground, several of the men had lots to say. Dart Philbun, who led the crew that broke into what is reported to be a burial chamber deep in the mine, said the most.

'It was a demon that came whooshing out of that small hole,' Philbun said. 'It boiled through that hole like steam and gasses and some slimy sticky goop that collected on the roof of the tunnel and turned into a huge glaring wolf. I told the men to run out of there and they did. I was the last one away from the tunnel face and thank God the evil smelling thing I can only call a demon didn't follow us. He just dropped to the floor of the tunnel and growled and let blood drip off his long white fangs as he stared at us with bright red eyes.'

Philbun said by the time he got to the lift shaft, men from other levels had heard about the demon and were talking about it. He went to the surface and reported the problem to the mine manager, who said he tried to play down the hole thing as just the product of the men's imagination.

The men milled around outside the mine at the shift change and a few men refused to go underground. When the day shift reported to work the next morning, only half the men showed up, effectively shutting down operation. Most men this reporter talked to agreed that there was a demon in the mine.

One said that when the night shift came off work those on the second level had to come out in total darkness. Sudden cold gusts of wind blew out every lantern and candle in the tunnel, and nobody could get any light started again. The men had to leave in total blackness.

A report from the same shift reported that on level four a tunnel had a small stream of water running between the tracks. During the middle of their shift, the men said the water reversed itself and began running in the opposite direction.

The change in direction of the water and the darkness of the other level were both said to be the work of the demon, warning them away from his domain.

Up to this time, no one has ventured underground to level two and to the end of the last drift to check on the breakthrough to determine what it actually is. Some report is expected within a week from the owner in San Francisco.

Morgan worked through the next three issues. They were essentially rewrites of the first story. The mine manager had not returned to the mine. He evidently was transferred or fired in San Francisco.

A local lawyer, P. Lawrence Kinnelly, had been named to handle all matters concerning the mine and its former employees. Mrs. Wheeler had not told Morgan that when she hired him.

Next stop, the law offices of P. Lawrence Kinnelly. Morgan found the office across from the bank on the second floor accessible by an outside stairs that led up from the boardwalk. He saw a sign on the door that said: "Come in," so he went in.

The office was plain, almost stark. No rug on the floor, not much varnish on the floorboards, tired paper on the walls and ceiling, and only two chairs and a desk in the ten-foot-square space.

A man behind the desk looked up without smiling.

"So?"

"Kinnelly?"

"Yes."

"I'm here from Mrs. Wheeler. She hired me to get this problem straightened out and the mine opened. What can you tell me about the situation here that wasn't in the newspaper reports?"

"Another one. She hired another damn detective." Kinnelly said it, threw down his pencil, and stood and walked over to the window that faced Main Street. He turned. Kinnelly was tall, broad, looked in good shape and had red hair, a face pocked with freckles and a beard that made a side-burns-wide swath down to his chin and ended in a classic Vandyke.

Morgan bet himself the man spent ten minutes every morning shaving the curving beard above and below to give the effect. It was the classy kind of beard Morgan often wished he'd take time to grow and maintain, but he couldn't be bothered.

"I told Mrs. Wheeler what needed doing. First get that damn Julio out of town, then go in with a solid crew and prove that the demon idea was a bunch of hogwash, and reopen the mine with anyone who wants to work. She'd have to pay a dollar more a day to get workers, but that would beat losing twenty thousand a month. Why are you here?"

"I'm going to get the mine open and take care of Julio. Now, like I said before, what can you tell me about the local situation, regarding the Lady Luck mine closure, that wasn't in the paper? Mostly I want to know who could benefit from closing down the mine."

Kinnelly scowled. "Nobody benefits from a closed-down mine. The workers lose out, the machinery rusts and gets lost, the stamping mill shuts down, the whole economy takes a jolt. Benefit? Maybe somebody who bought the mine cheap if and when Mrs. Wheeler decided to sell it. Which she won't. You must have met her. She's an old rapscallion and tough as a twenty-penny nail in a cherry pie."

Morgan grinned. "Agreed. Now, is there an adjoining mine around owned by a man who's ambitious and might pull a stunt like this?"

"Not within fifty miles. Most of these mines started with a pick and a shovel and two friends. No big money up here on most of these mines."

"So you think this demon thing is all a hoax?"

"Didn't say that. Never have said that. I don't make judgments without knowing all the facts. I haven't been underground to check on this demon cavern. Don't aim to go."

"How does Julio fit in?"

"He caught the fancy of the granddaughter, Alexis. Came up here to be a manager of some kind in a mine, but he said the offer fell through. He had some experience up here years ago when the mines first opened."

"So he's working for another mine.?"

"No. He's just sitting and waiting. Opened an

office, Mountain Mining. No visible means of support, the police would say."

"Is the girl with him?"

"She is. I take it Mrs. Wheeler wants you to snatch the girl and take her back to San Francisco."

"Persuade would be a better term. Do that and take Julio back to face a charge of kidnapping."

"Won't work. I told Mrs. Wheeler. Alexis is past eighteen. Was when she came up here with Julio. That's an empty threat and Julio knows it."

"Are they married?"

"Not that I know of."

"Living together?"

"As far as I know. That's not illegal either."

"What happened to T. J. Fox?"

The lawyer frowned and sat down in his desk chair. He waved Morgan to the other chair. "He couldn't cope with the demon problem, so he quit or got fired, I don't know which. That's why I'm holding down the reins here for the time being."

Morgan stood, his mind made up. "Good, tonight you and I have an appointment. Wear clothes you don't mind getting dirty, bring two coal oil lamps and lots of matches. Tonight you and I are going to go into the Lady Luck mine and find that burial cave and shake hands with the demon, if he's still there."

"Hey, hey, don't include me in your insanity."

"You'll come, or I'll tell Mrs. Wheeler that you can't do the job she hired you for. We'll meet at your office at midnight. Don't be late. I'll have a pair of horses we can ride out there. It's only a mile, but that time of night a horse will be handy. Oh, bring along a six-gun if you have one, or borrow a shotgun and a whole pocketful of double-aught buck rounds. We might need them for a demon, or just some practical joking guy who is counting on getting gold-mine rich."

The lawyer scowled again. "Then you think it's only some man or a couple of men out there staging all these demon things?"

"Might be. I have an explanation for the first sighting that could be right. I need to look around a little first. The rest of it could be explained away by fear and panic. Midnight. I'll see you then."

Morgan turned and walked out of the office before the lawyer could make an objection.

At the foot of the stairs, he asked the first person who came along which direction Apple Street was. The young matron pointed down the street to his left and continued on with only a polite smile.

He found Apple Street and saw that 310 would be in the third block from Main. By now Morgan figured he had enough background on the caper to have a talk with the lady in question, Alexis Wheeler. That is he would if she was at 310 Apple Street, Apartment B, and if she would talk to him.

He had no thought that Alexis was being held captive, but there probably would be someone with her. Not a guard exactly, but someone to stay with her, be with her.

He found 310 Apple and saw that the one time one-family house had been cut into two units. The new door at the near side had a letter "B" on it. He went up a hint of a walkway and knocked on the panel.

Nothing happened. He knocked again, eight times, each with increasing power.

A moment later the door opened an inch and he saw an eye and little else.

"What do you want?" a male voice asked.

"I've come to visit Alexis."

"Nobody here by that name," the same male

voice said. There was a tremor in the words. Morgan didn't believe him.

"Just tell her that I'm here as a friend and I won't take up much of her time."

"I told you . . ."

At that point, Morgan kicked the door with the sole of his right boot and the door slammed open, knocking the speaker backwards so hard that he fell to the floor.

Morgan stepped into the opening with his six-gun drawn. "Hold it right there, friend," Morgan rasped. "I don't want to shoot anybody my first day in town."

The man on the floor was the same small, dark man Morgan had talked with in the Mountain Mining office.

"Get up and take me to Alexis or I might have to get unpleasant."

"That won't be necessary, whoever you are. I'm right behind you." It was a soft feminine voice that was neutral, neither angry or happy.

Morgan turned slowly expecting at least a shotgun to be aimed at him. Instead he saw a sweet-faced girl with flowing midnight black hair and a sleek young body in men's pants and a blouse tucked in at the waist. She wasn't smiling.

"What do you mean breaking into my home this way? And put down that silly gun. No one is going to hurt you."

"No one? Then why did somebody take two shots at me not two hours ago?"

She frowned. "Someone shot at you? Must have been a mistake. Grandmother sent you, didn't she? Just like the last two. I told her not to. I write her every week. She just won't understand."

"You came up here with Julio of your own free will?"

"Of course. What did she tell you, that he kidnapped me? I'm eighteen, I can do as I please."

"True. You can also break the heart of a little old lady who raised you like you were her own child."

"I'm sorry about that, but I have my own life to live." She sat down in one of the chairs in the room and motioned him into another one. The small man on the floor had stood and waited near the door.

"Does Mrs. Wheeler expect you to take over her empire and run it as a Wheeler should?"

The hint of a smile lightened Alexis's face. "Something like that. She wanted me to go to some fancy women's college. I don't want to be all that 'educated.' I just want a husband and a home and a family. Is that asking too much?"

"So Julio is your intended. Have you married him?"

"No, not yet. He's waiting for some business deal to come through."

"Are you living with him?"

Her face flared red with anger. "Of course not! How could you even ask me such a thing?"

"Then why not wait for him back in San Francisco? There doesn't seem to be much to entertain a person up here in Hangtown."

"I want to be here."

"Who is your keeper?" Morgan motioned at the man near the door.

"His name is Fernando and he works for Julio. Yes, he is my protector. This is sometimes a wild and rough little town."

Morgan turned his brown low-crowned Stetson around and around in his hands. "Alexis, I agree with you. You have every right to be up here with your intended. Still, it does seem a little unfriendly just to run out on your grandmother that way. She did raise you since the time you were four."

"I know, I know. She keeps throwing that up at me every time we talk."

"You are her only living relative."

"I don't want her money if that's what you're getting around to. I don't believe I even know your name."

"Sorry, my manners. I'm Lee Morgan."

Her head turned quickly and she stared at him; then her face warmed into a soft smile and she was beautiful.

"Morgan? You're Lee Buckskin Morgan? Grandma has been keeping track of you for years. I think she had a wild love affair with your father back many years ago. Well, I am surprised."

"I was flabbergasted when I learned that your grandmother knew my father. It's a small world sometimes. Have you considered going back to San Francisco for a visit?"

"No, she'd do something to make me stay. My place is here, to be near Julio."

"Yes, Julio. I haven't met him yet. Perhaps you could introduce me to him one of these days."

"That might be possible." She watched him. "Now, Mr. Morgan, if there's nothing else . . ."

"There is one other thing. Julio is waiting on a business deal. Does it involve his buying a mine?"

She looked up quickly. "That's a private matter. Even if his business involved a mine, I couldn't say anything about it."

"Most working mines are not for sale. I was wondering which one it was?"

"Sorry. Now I'd appreciate it if you would leave. I have nothing more to say to you."

"Yes, I think you're right. Why am I thinking that Julio is trying to get hold of your grandmother's mine, the Lady Luck? Now with the trouble up there it might be sold at a low price. I'm just thinking. When did Julio come up to the mountain?"

"About four months ago, why?"

"Two months after the mine shut down. Just curious, Miss Wheeler. Just curious."

Morgan headed for the door. The small man there backed up giving him room. At the door, Morgan turned and looked at Alexis.

"Miss Wheeler. When you see Julio, you might tell him I'm in town, and I'm most anxious to meet him."

"Mr. Morgan, if you're that anxious to meet me, turn around slowly, I'm right behind you and my own .45 is aimed at your spine, so don't even make a flicker of a motion toward your hogleg."

Chapter Four

Lee Morgan turned slowly, as Julio suggested. He saw a medium-sized man standing beside Alexis, his six-gun trained on Morgan in a steady hand. The man was five-ten, slight, with a dark Mexican cast to his skin, black hair, black moustache, and dark eyes. He wore a red leather vest over a brown shirt and brown town pants and fancy tooled cowboy boots.

"Now that you've met me, Morgan, get out and leave us alone. Tell Mrs. Wheeler we don't want to have anything to do with her."

Morgan laughed. "You put up a big front, my small friend. You talk a good game, but when the showdown comes, we'll see how you change your tune. I've handled a dozen no-goods like you before. You've already made too many mistakes; it's almost time to pay up.

"Like this afternoon from that alley. You or one of your gunmen missed me. Should have been an

easy shot, but the bushwhacker got nervous and
stood back too far. He must have been afraid to
look the man he was going to murder in the eye.
Was that man you, Julio?"

"Get out, now." The words came low and furious.
Julio lowered the weapon, perhaps so he wouldn't
be tempted to use it. Morgan saw the hatred in the
black eyes and nodded.

"Anything you say, gunman. You've got the per-
suader. Next time you might not be able to draw
when my back's turned." He heard the gasp from
the Mexican as he opened the door and went outside.

Morgan walked stiffly down the path to the
street, half expecting a rifle round in his back at
any moment. Julio had been so mad he couldn't
think straight. That was good. When they were in
the wrong, most men got angry.

Curious how Julio reacted to the shooting story.
Perhaps he wasn't the gunman. But he knew about
the attempt. Once out of range, Morgan slowed his
walk and angled up Main Street. The place was
speckled with saloons and gambling halls. At the
next one he came to, Morgan went in and asked
for a mug of beer at the bar.

The apron drew one and shoved it down the
counter. Morgan saw the sign and spun a dime
up the bar toward the keep.

The place serviced mostly drinkers, but there
were half a dozen tables for card games. Only one
game played with four chairs filled.

Morgan listened for any gossip or rumors about
the Lady Luck. He didn't even hear the name of
the mine mentioned and nothing about demons
or spells or curses.

After an hour of nursing his beer and watching
the bad play of the poker game, Morgan gave up

and went to find some supper. The cafe where he
had lunch was named The Mule Cafe. He hadn't
noticed that before. He went back in and ordered
a steak dinner and asked the waitress about the
name.

"Oh, that. We should change it. When the place
first started out sometimes the only meat we
had was mule, so the customers named the
place. Nobody has got around to changing the
name yet."

The steak was definitely beef, and cooked
medium-rare, the way he liked it, with side dishes
and a small loaf of bread and salted fresh butter.

After the meal, Morgan went to the livery and
had them saddle up two riding horses. He led the
horses down the street and tied them to a hitching
rail at the side of the White Quartz Hotel, then
went inside. Morgan checked at the hotel desk,
found no messages in his box, picked up his key
and went up to his room. That was when he realized that Helen Curley wasn't at the desk.

Morgan grinned. She'd be around later. He
would have time to write down a few things in his
notebook about the case. It was starting to become
a reality to him and already he had met some of
the players. He wasn't forgetting his date with the
lawyer to check out the mine at midnight.

Morgan stood to the wall side of his door on
the second floor, turned the key in the lock and
heard no gunfire from inside the room. Good. He
pushed the door open inward with enough force
to swing it against the wall. Nobody hiding behind
the door.

By that time it was starting to get dark and
the room showed in various shades of gray and
black. The hall lamp from two doors down cast
only a soft light through the door. Morgan stepped

inside, found the lamp on the dresser and lit it, then closed the door and locked it.

"About damn time you got here," a woman's voice said behind him.

He spun around, his right hand busy with the lamp so he was unable to draw. He grinned when he saw the woman spread out on the bed wearing only a thin chemise and nothing else.

"I've been waiting for you, Big Balls Morgan. What took you so long?"

Morgan's brow went up and then he chortled. "Anticipation, my dear, it always turns making love into a delight."

She slid off the bed, the chemise not covering the triangle of blonde fur tracking down her little mound to her crotch. Helen's big breasts bounded and rolled under the thin chemise. She walked to him and pushed hard against him from hips to chest and then reached up and kissed his lips.

"I've been anticipating this for two hours. I just hope like hell it's as good as it looks like it's gonna be."

He kissed both her eyes, then ripped the chemise from neckline to hem and pushed it back from her breasts. Her eyes went wide a minute; then she pushed against him, her bare breasts hard against his chest.

"Oh, damn but that makes me go wild." She pulled him toward the bed. "I was gonna be shy and slow, but damn it, I can't wait." She knelt in front of him and unbuttoned his fly, then looked up. "Pull him out, right now, I can't wait!"

Morgan worked inside and a minute later had his full blown erection pushing out of his buckskins.

Her eyes went wide, then her lips parted. "My god, so big, so perfect!" She went down on him, kissing his rod, then licking the purple tip and at last sucking him into her mouth. Helen bounced up and down on his cock a dozen times, then slid away and stood and pulled Morgan to the bed.

"Right now, Morgan. Fuck me right now before I explode!" She fell on the bed on her back, spread her legs and then lifted her knees almost to her chest, exposing her pink slot.

"Right now, Morgan. Don't even take your pants off. I like it a little scratchy and rough sometimes."

Morgan went between her legs and lowered. In one deft thrust he sank his manhood up to his pubic bones in her. Helen grunted, then whispered and crooned at the juncture. Her legs came up high over his back; then her ankles locked and her hips began to pound upward at him with each of his strokes. His town pants scraped her tender flesh with each thrust but she didn't complain.

She began to gasp almost from the start. Then she changed to a soft moaning and her mouth sought his. She cried out then, a long wailing keening that Morgan figured penetrated the thin hotel walls like a knife through butter.

Without warning she stopped. Morgan frowned, stopped thrusting and looked at her. "Are you all right?"

She grinned. "Fuck yes! I just wanted to make it last longer. Can you chew on my tits? They feel left out."

He bent and chewed on each of her flattened breasts. Spread out the way they were, they still were bigger than those of lots of other women Morgan had bedded. He nibbled on her nipples, then bit each one and pounded one hard stroke into her.

"Oh, yes," Helen squealed. "Do me now."

Morgan went to his knees and elbows and slammed hard into her willing form. With each power thrust she pounded back at him and on the exchange she moved another inch up the bed.

Ten hard strokes later he could feel the heat coming from her. She wrapped her arms around him and met him with a hard hip thrust for each of his. Then she exploded.

Her face distorted with the thunderous climax. Her whole body went rigid; then her hips vibrated and shook like she was going to come apart. Her whole body spasmed as half the voluntary muscles in her body contracted again and again as the tremors powered through her. She closed her eyes and went with the spasms, tracking them, blessing them, then feeling them rattle on out of her body.

At last she gave one last sigh and fell back to the mattress as limp as yesterday's cut flowers.

Her eyes snapped open. "Oh, my, that was beautiful. Now, sweet Morgan, it's your turn. Come on, you were almost there before, I sensed it."

He took no second invitation. He jolted into her again, with long deep thrusts that set his blood on fire. He clenched his teeth as he felt the juices almost ready to blast down his tubes. Six more thrusts and then the gates broke and the fluids rushed out and down the tube and spurted hard and deep from the tip of his penis.

Morgan growled and roared as the spurts came one after another. The last one he powered hard and held it as he pinned her halfway into the mattress. When he relaxed and let her lift back to the top of the mattress, he lay gently on top of her form, using her breasts as twin pillows, and panted like the steam engine of the decade had just been installed in his gut.

When it was over, she held him again, her arms clamped around him, tying them together. A wonderful smile wreathed her face and her lips sang a little soundless tune.

When Morgan revived, she let loose of him and he pulled away from her and lay beside her on his back, still gasping now and then to help replace the used-up energy of the coupling.

"I hope you liked it," Helen said, leaning up on one arm so she could look at him. "It was fantastic for me."

"Wait until the third time before you say that," Morgan advised. "That way it has to get better every time."

"Three times, tonight?"

"Sure, before midnight. I have a late appointment."

She sat up, making her big breasts bounce and jiggle. Morgan watched them in wonder. He'd seen big ones before, but these were so young and firm *and* big.

"What do you mean, you have a midnight appointment? You going to another woman?"

"After three rounds with you? Not a chance. I've got some work to do late tonight."

"Oh." She pouted, her lips extending, eyes wary. She crossed her arms under her breasts. "What kind of work?"

"Hard work," Morgan said. "Why don't you undress me."

She looked at him. "What?"

"Strip my clothes off. Haven't you ever wanted to do that to a man?"

"Well, sure, sometimes."

"How about now?" He bent and nibbled on her nipple, then licked it and kissed around one of her breasts.

"Yeah, like now."

She undressed him slowly, working at it as an erotic dance, working up to pulling down his shorts in one rush to leave him completely naked. When she jerked down his underwear his short arm was long again, hard as a pine tree and sticking up at an inviting angle. She chortled.

"I want to be on top this time."

She was.

It was long and slow and by the time they were rested up after that second encounter, Morgan checked his watch. It was eleven-thirty. He slid off the bed and started putting on his clothes.

"What the fuck you doing? You said three times."

"Sorry, we had so much fun it turned out to be twice. Now hold onto your tits, girl. I'll be back. There's always tomorrow night or maybe tomorrow afternoon. We have lots of time yet to work out those other twenty positions you wanted to try. Right?"

He petted her breasts and her frown turned slowly into a grin. "The girls and me are waiting for you. 'Cepting I better get to my own room. Figure you won't be back anytime like reasonable tonight."

"Probably not until daylight."

He finished dressing and she moved around on the bed in provocative poses trying to trick him into staying. When she saw that it didn't work, she walked on her knees across the bed and hugged him, her breasts flattening against his chest.

"Hey, Morgan, you best fucker. When you get back tonight or tomorrow, will you do me a back door? Nobody ever done me a back door. Just want to see how it feels."

"Back door?"

"You know, my other hole down there."

"We'll see when we get to it. Now, get dressed so I can leave."

"You can leave anytime. I won't steal none of your goods. Remember I have a passkey. I can get in anytime I want to anyhow."

Morgan nodded, kissed her softly on the lips and left the room carrying his six-gun in his holster and the Spencer 7-shot rifle over his shoulder.

"Look like you're going bear hunting."

Morgan laughed. "That's exactly what we may find, a damned bear." With that he closed the door behind him and hurried down the hall.

The two horses were where he had tied them. He rode one and led the other down the street to the lawyer's office. The man came out of the shadows next to his stairway.

"Didn't know if you'd come or not," Kinnelly said. He wore old pants, a wool shirt and a battered hat. He also now had a gunbelt with a six-gun sticking out of worn leather.

"No shotgun?" Morgan asked.

Before Morgan could move, Kinnelly whipped up a sawed-off shotgun that he had tied to a cord around his neck. "I try to be ready for any kind of situation," the lawyer said. He picked up two kerosene lanterns from the shadows and passed one to Morgan, took one himself and mounted the horse.

Morgan nodded and they rode out of town south, away from the Lady Luck.

Kinnelly grinned in the moonlight. "Figured we'd come this way first, then circle around to the Lady Luck. I can tell you I don't have the slightest idea what we're going to find out there tonight. Not altogether happy about going, but I know it's part of my job. What the hell, a guy can only get fried or exploded by a demon once."

"I get the feeling this demon might be something more natural than we might suspect. You have a plan of the mine with a level map?"

"Yep. Figured you wouldn't have one. What we want is level two. We go in the main entrance and back that tunnel for about fifty yards where we get to the main shaft. There's a bucket, but also ladders on four sides for those going down just one level. The main shaft goes down for over a hundred feet, so we better check those rungs as we make our way down."

Morgan agreed. "No sense getting sloppy so early in the game. My guess is that we should leave our horses about a hundred yards from the guard shack. Chances are the old man will be snoring away. I want to check to see if there's a pint of whiskey somewhere near the entrance to the mine."

Kinnelly laughed. "He told you that story, too? Best chance for that pint is that it winds up in the gut of that watchman and the empty gets pitched down a canyon somewhere. Makes a fine story but I wouldn't believe that old coot."

"You know him?"

"Been around town longer than I have. He's a survivor. No matter what happens he seems to land on his feet, scratching and clawing for his pay."

Fifteen minutes later, they tied their horses to some brush down from the guard shack and walked ahead silently. A coal oil lamp flickered on the last drops of fuel in the glass bowl. The watchman sat in his chair, head fallen to his chest, an empty whiskey bottle still in his hand.

They went past silently and edged up to the side of the walled-off front of the mine. A man-sized door in the big plug swung a foot open. There was a hasp and pin available but evidently no one had thought to lock it.

Morgan picked up the pin and threw it 30 yards into the brush. They worked the door open another foot and listened inside. Then both stepped through the opening quickly, into the blackness.

Morgan flicked on a match and lit his lantern. The sudden light hurt his eyes a moment.

"We'll use one lantern at a time," he whispered to Kinnelly. They looked around at the entrance to the mine. The tunnel was more than a head high, cut wide with a set of rails down the center for ore cars.

On workdays there probably would be kerosene-soaked torches along the tunnel to give a little light. They moved forward along the tracks. Twenty feet into the tunnel they came to the first drift, another tunnel dug back into the side to explore the chances of finding a seam of quartz and gold.

This drift ran only ten feet and stopped. They moved forward again, checking each drift, watching for any sign of someone living in the tunnels—food, garbage, sleeping places. They found nothing to indicate anyone had been staying in the mine.

Fifty yards along the main tunnel, they came to sturdy four-by-fours set in the ground supporting a solid fence of two-by-sixes. The front side of the fence was a removable gate to make loading the ore easier into the ore cars. One ore car sat there, half-filled, with two shovels abandoned nearby.

Morgan looked carefully around the shaft in the half-inch of dust that had settled. He found nothing but a few rat tracks. No boot prints.

Near the shaft rested a tool rack with all sorts of tools—wrenches, wire, a pair of lanterns, a box of matches, and some of the newfangled head lamps that attached to the miner's helmet. At one side lay half a dozen lengths of rope. Morgan took one of them, tied the lantern to it and lowered it down the shaft. Twelve feet below, he saw where the shaft widened and a new tunnel had been carved out of the mountain.

Morgan tied off the rope holding the lantern to the top rung of the ladder, then moved down hand over hand to the level below. As he went he tested each of the rungs. All were solid and sure.

Kinnelly came next with his lantern hooked over one arm. Morgan untied the lit lantern and held up his hands.

"Which way?" he whispered. The sound came out much louder than Morgan had intended. Then he realized that every sound in the tunnel was amplified and echoed down the length of the tube.

Kinnelly pointed the opposite direction they had been going, back to the outside of the mountain, and they walked around an empty ore car on the tracks and then walked between the rails.

An icy blast of air whistled past them and Kinnelly shivered.

"What the hell was that?" he whispered.

"Not a demon," Morgan whispered back. "Air heats and cools in tunnels like this. Often it blows from one area to another to equalize the pressure. Happens all the time underground."

They walked ahead. Kinnelly had told Morgan that the target tunnel on level two was only 50 yards long. It was a searching probe trying to uncover some more veins of the gold-bearing quartz.

Morgan sensed that they were almost to the end. He felt a change in the air temperature, then smelled something he couldn't identify. It was almost like the smell of a decomposed body but it had another quality to it.

Behind him, Kinnelly smelled the odor too. "It's the damn demon!" He turned and bolted away from the light. Morgan charged after him, grabbed him from behind and spun him around.

"Kinnelly! Get hold of yourself. It's just a smell. There's not a damn thing to worry about."

Kinnelly's face was a mask of fear. "I can see something back there. Look!" His voice had risen to a shriek. Before Morgan could stop him, the lawyer pulled a six-inch hunting knife from his belt and threw it down the dark tunnel.

The next second Morgan heard the knife hit the rocks of the tunnel. Suddenly sparks fly and the far end of the rocky tube exploded with a roar of deadly flames.

Chapter Five

The roaring flames in the tunnel burned out in a horrendous pair of seconds. The force of the blast knocked down both Morgan and the lawyer. The shock wave tore the lantern from Morgan's hand and blew out the flame. The two men lay on the floor of the tunnel panting for breath in the sudden and total darkness of what certainly must be hell.

"Kinnelly, you all right? Any broken bones, burned-off clothes, like that?"

The reply came out of the darkness near at hand. "I'm alive, Morgan. I hurt too much to be dead. Christ, what the hell was that?"

"An explosion of some kind. Now don't try to tell me that it was the demon. We were almost to the end and I saw no evidence of anything supernatural whatsoever."

Vaguely Morgan realized the panic run by Kinnelly had probably saved their lives, since it had moved them farther away from the blast.

The darkness pressed in on him like a tomb. Morgan sat up on the cold dirt of the tunnel floor and felt in his pocket for matches. He remembered bringing plenty.

"Damn it, Morgan, let's get the hell out of here. I'm hurting. I'm also scared as hell and I don't mind admitting it. I just got blown off my feet and I think half my hair is burned off and my face feels like a fried steak."

"You know where your lantern is?"

"No."

Morgan lit two matches, striking them on the steel rails. For just a fraction of a second he hoped the burning match wouldn't cause another blast. He held his breath as the matches flared but there was no new explosion. Morgan found his lantern where he had dropped it during the blast. The whoosh of air had blown out the flame. Then in the light of the match he saw that the glass lens around the lamp had shattered.

He checked the fuel. It sloshed in the tank. Good. Morgan pushed the match through the broken glass and lit the wick, then rolled it up a little and the new greater light leaped into the darkness, eating it up for a dozen feet around them.

Kinnelly found his lantern where the shock wave had rolled it. The glass in his was intact. He lit the wick and they both stood up.

Again the flare of the new match had brought no explosion, only blessed light. Kinnelly dropped the glass lens back in place and moved the light toward his face.

"My eyes feel all right. How's my face and hair?" Kinnelly asked. The man's hat had been blown off and his hair was singed. But it didn't look serious. The burns on his face were only red, not blistered as they could have been.

Morgan's hat had remained in place. He looked at his hands and saw red welts and minor burns on both. Morgan motioned down the tracks toward the shaft.

"We better get out of here and come back later. We learned a few things on the trip. Oh, Kinnelly, I don't want you to say a word about what we did here tonight and especially nothing about that fire and explosion. You hear. Not one single word. We got burned in a small fire, that's all. I don't want this ridiculous wave of panic about the demon to get any more ammunition. You understand?"

"Yes, of course. I know the value of not blabbing my business all over town."

They walked out of the mine in record time.

Kinnelly threw his arms wide and embraced the open air.

"I can assure you, sir, that I will never in my future life on this planet, ever, ever go into a mine again. No tunnels, no drifts, no shafts. Not ever again!"

They walked past the guard shack and saw the watchman still sleeping. He'd dropped the whiskey bottle, and the lantern had nearly burned out of fuel. They didn't bother waking him.

It was after two A.M. before Morgan turned in the horses at the livery and got to his hotel room. He was registered in 212. He checked the place, found that Helen Curley had indeed returned to her own bed. Morgan looked in the room across the hall. It was unoccupied. His key had opened the door. He moved his guns and carpet bag into Room 213, locked the door and put the straight-backed chair under the door knob.

If anyone tried to get in they would have to break the chair first and by then Morgan would be ready for them. He often rented one room and slept in another. If anyone had the thought to bomb his room or rake it with double aught buck, his moving out gave him a life-saving advantage.

Morgan slept at once, awoke once when some raucous rooster announced that dawn was breaking at 6:45. He went back to sleep until eight, got up and started to shave. He stopped before his razor hit his face. His face was slightly swollen and had several red spots on it. He dug out his small jar of aloe vera cream and dabbed it on the red spots. At once they felt better.

He had picked up the cream in Mexico, and found it beat anything he'd ever tried on burns. The backs of his hands were slightly worse. He spread the cream on them as well and the stinging faded away.

Morgan put on a pair of town pants and brown town shirt and a brown vest. His buckskins were dirty from the mine explosion.

He went for breakfast, decided to eat in the hotel dining room and had just settled down to a stack of hotcakes, bacon, country fries and coffee when Helen stopped at his table.

"Is the service here satisfactory, Mr. Morgan?" Her dark blue eyes twinkled at the double meaning of her question.

"Everything is better than fine, Miss Curley. I appreciate you inquiring. These hotcakes are great."

"Did you sleep well, Mr. Morgan?"

"I did have some interruptions, early in the evening, but when I got to sleep, I was like a babe in a crib."

Again she smiled and nodded. "Mr. Morgan, we hope your stay here will be pleasant. If there is anything I can do for you, just leave a sealed note for me at the desk."

She grinned wickedly and went on to another table that had four for breakfast. Morgan delighted in watching the pronounced sway of her hips under the skirt as she walked. Then he got back to business.

First on his agenda for the day was a talk with the former top foreman in the mine, Karl Bullitt. His position and address were in the material that Mrs. Wheeler had given him in San Francisco. There was a note that mentioned Karl as the most loyal of all the Lady Luck workers.

Morgan found him home. He had been pacing the living room at his small, neat home when Morgan arrived.

"Heard somebody was in town about the mine," Bullitt said. "I been wondering when you'd come and talk."

Morgan introduced himself and they sat down on worn furniture. Bullitt leaned forward.

"When can we start up the mine again, Mr. Morgan?"

"I'm hoping within a week, two at the most." Morgan paused. "Then I'd say you're not worried about the demon out there?"

"Not a bit. I wasn't there, but I know a couple of the men who were. A bunch of stupid men who will believe anything somebody wants them to. Maybe they were tired of working long hours. Me, I want to get back to work."

"How many of the crew could you get to go underground?"

Bullitt stood, walked to the door, and came back rubbing his jaw in thought. "Damn, that could be a problem. I'd guess full half of the men still won't go underground."

"So before we open the mine, we have to convince them that either the demon never existed, and explain what the men down there saw and explain away the water flow and the lamps blowing out, or we have to prove the demon has been sealed up in the end of that tunnel and is trapped and can't work any more of his deadly trickery."

Bullitt bobbed his head. "Yeah, about the way I see it. How we going to do one or the other?"

"Doesn't matter to you which way?" Morgan asked.

"Not a bit. Either way."

Morgan stood and shook Bullitt's hand. "Now we're making some progress. Can you find me twenty good men who can do what they're told and keep their mouths shut? Won't be anything illegal or even hateful. I just need some men I can count on to help me when the time comes."

"Twenty? Damn yes! I can get twenty before nighttime. You just tell me where you want us and how many and what tools or equipment we need and we'll be there roaring to go. Most of us men been out of work longer than we want to be."

Morgan shook hands with the man again, then headed uptown. Before he got halfway along Main Street, he heard the story everywhere. The demon had struck again. It had blasted two men in the same tunnel on level two, burned them severely and chased them out of the tunnel roaring and spitting flames at them all the way.

Morgan growled to himself. He shouldn't have taken Kinnelly with him last night. Now there was one more happening that he'd have to disprove.

Julio sat at the kitchen table in the house where Alexis Wheeler lived. He had just finished a noon meal and he was tapping his fingers on the table as he tried to work out a new plan. The news about the lawyer and somebody else going into the tunnel last night and being met with a fiery welcome had been a stroke of luck.

He couldn't explain it and he didn't try. It was one more nail in the casket that would bury the Lady Luck. He had to get a few more nails in place. He had an idea that he had worked on before. Now he realized that the fire-breathing demon from last night would fit into his plan like a hand in a glove.

He grinned and began making more notes on the pad of paper on the table. He sipped coffee and looked over at Alexis. She knew nothing of what he was doing, and that was fine. Either way it would work out well. At the proper time he would marry the girl, and be the co-heir to the fifty million dollars and all of the property that Alexis's grandmother owned in San Francisco.

Julio had hoped that the old woman would die quickly. He was afraid if he married Alexis before the woman died, she and her lawyers would work out some plan so all of her money went to some kind of charity. The problem still rankled him.

He had come to the mountains partly to get away from the old woman, but also so he could see what kind of magic he could work on the Lady Luck mine. It was a perfect setup for him. Two of the important elements were already in place. The problem would be the stubbornness of Wilma Wheeler back there in San Francisco.

He worked on his plan again. It could take place just above the town on the forward slopes of the mountain. There was a large cleared area where the loggers had cut down every tree large enough to form timbers for the various mines. That cleared spot was more than 500 yards square. It would work perfectly.

Julio checked to be sure that his man had brought back the right equipment from Sacramento. Most of it was not available there in Hangtown. Anyway, he didn't want any tie between him or his man and buying such equipment.

Yes, it should work. He would plan it in three days. Now that he was in the homestretch, he couldn't get too anxious. Slow and steady and he would come out in the clover.

He had to promote and prove the existence of the demon. So far the townspeople and most of the Lady Luck workers had only the tall tales of someone else. He had to give them a personal display of the demon's power. He had to build up the demon so strong that Mrs. Wheeler would agree to sell. That was the snag. Everything could go well here and then Mrs. Wheeler could back out of any deal. She could afford to.

Julio smiled. He did have one joker he could play if she would not sign. He had Alexis. He could offer to return Alexis to San Francisco and convince her to stay there—but only if Mrs. Wheeler would sell him the Lady Luck mine for ten dollars. It would be pure blackmail, but it should work. The old woman wanted her granddaughter back, and she would give up the mine to get her.

If the deal worked he'd never tell Alexis about the mine. He'd convince her that it would be best for now for her to return to San Francisco and to her grandmother. It would be temporary. In a year or so her grandmother would forget her anger at Julio and then he could sweep into San Francisco and marry her and they would live happily ever after with at least six children, three boys and three girls. He knew that she would go along.

If Mrs. Wheeler balked at trading the girl for the mine, he could threaten to rape and ruin Alexis, spread the story to the San Francisco papers, and Alexis would not be the darling of the social set that she had become. It would also kill any kind of a socially acceptable marriage at all for dear Alexis.

The old woman would bow under that kind of pressure and trade the mine for her beloved grand-daughter. It would be a fine trade. Alexis would be safe in San Francisco and he'd run the mine. Then after a year or so, when Mrs. Wheeler took her last breath, Julio would charge into town and marry the girl.

But first he had to start winning over the people of Hangtown, and especially the men who worked in the mine. He had to build up the demon, then be the hero and defeat the demon and blast him closed into the end of the tunnel. He made more lines on a drawing of the mountain behind the town. He estimated the cost and decided the gamble would be worth it. He began making a new list of materials. He had almost doubled the size of the demonstration. The larger the better. He would send his man to Sacramento again with a wagon and a good team. He'd have to travel all day and night to get there and get back in time.

Morgan had his noon meal at the Mule Cafe. He had just stepped out on the boardwalk when he saw Alexis come from the General Store and head toward her rented house. He fell into step beside her.

"Miss Wheeler? Would it be all right if I walked you home? Some of these miners get wild even at midday."

"I'm perfectly capable of taking care of myself," she said. He saw her glance at him from the side of her eyes. She hadn't said no.

He shortened his steps to match hers. "Fine day," he said.

"Yes."

"Good old summertime."

"That's the time of year."

"Winters up here are extremely cold."

"I've been told." She stopped and stared at him. "Mr. Morgan, there is no way that you can talk your way into my favor. I know you're here with orders from Grandmother, and I am sure she wants you to bring me back to San Francisco. So don't even be nice to me."

Morgan chuckled. "I have no orders to kidnap you and whisk you back to the coast. On the other hand, I'm a fool for a pretty face and a fine figure and I truly do enjoy talking with intelligent women. Is that such a surprise to you?"

She frowned, looking as if she didn't know quite how to respond to the compliments.

"So, I saw you and decided on the spur of the moment to walk you home. In broad daylight, what can it hurt?"

"Nothing, Mr. Morgan. Just be aware, I am on to your little games. Julio is a wonderful man and he loves me and he wants to marry me and some day we will become man and wife. Grandmother will just have to accept that."

"You've known Julio for some time?"

"More than seven months now. He was at some of the society affairs that Grandmother sponsored, charity things, to help the poor and homeless. We danced, I enjoyed being with him. Three months later we came up here. I am going to marry him."

"No argument. You sure do sparkle when you get mad that way. Gives your face a kind of vitality and pertness. Mighty pretty."

"Stop saying things like that. I'm engaged, I'm promised. Julio is my intended. How else can I say it so you'll understand?"

"You know much about Julio? What kind of profession or occupation does he have?"

"He invests in various business ventures. He grew up in San Francisco, the way I did. I've never met any of his family. In case you're wondering, he's not Mexican, he's Spanish. His parents came to San Francisco over fifty years ago. His father was the Alcalde of San Francisco."

They came to the end of the boardwalk with only the dirt of the street ahead. She stepped off the eight-inch drop and lost her balance, her arms flailed and she caught at him. Morgan wrapped both arms around her and kept her from falling. Her breasts pressed hard against his chest.

"Oh dear!" she yelped. Then she nodded. "Thank you for saving me from the dust. I so hate all the dust and dirt up here."

She frowned. "Mr. Morgan, I have regained my balance. You can let go of me now."

He held her just a moment longer. "Oh, I figured that was my reward."

She shot an angry glance at him.

"I was only teasing you. I have a rule of never touching a pretty lady unless she wants me to."

Alexis harumphed. "Just how do you know when she wants you to touch her?"

"There are ways. I've learned the little signals you ladies give out sometimes whether you want to or not. But enough of that. I wanted to tell you that part of my job while I'm here is to reopen your grandmother's mine, the Lucky Lady. I'll be involved in that for some time, if I don't see you again for a few days."

They had arrived at her door. Alexis nodded. Before she could open the door, the small dark man Morgan had seen there before swung the panel open. In his hand he held a six-gun. He quickly pushed it behind his back.

"Welcome home, señorita," he said—his accent thicker now than when Morgan had talked to him at the downtown office.

Alexis frowned at the small man, then turned to Morgan. Her smile seemed a little forced but was grand. He had the feeling she was being nice to him to spite her guard.

"Mr. Morgan, it was so kind of you to see me home. I appreciate it. Perhaps we'll meet again sometime."

Morgan smiled. "It's a small town, Miss Wheeler. I'm sure we'll see each other again before long."

Morgan turned and walked quickly away from the house, well aware of the surprise and anger building in the small Mexican guard. It wasn't time to deal with him. Not yet.

Chapter Six

Morgan stepped up to the boardwalk at the end of Main Street and saw a strange procession coming toward him. He waited and soon realized the six people were all in church robes. Leading them was a Catholic priest in his black and purple cassock. At each side walked an altar boy, carrying two-foot–high crosses. Behind them came three mourners draped in black, with sackcloth across their shoulders and soot marking their faces.

The priest held two books, one a well-worn Bible and another a slender volume that had a shiny new cover.

Morgan watched them go by and stopped a man walking down the boardwalk.

"Who are they and where are they going?" Morgan asked, pointing to the group.

The man snorted. "Bunch of damn foolishness you ask me. That's Father Rinaldi from the Catholic church. He's going to try to exorcise the demon out of the mine. He's convinced that he can do it." The man shook his head and continued on his way.

Exorcise the demon out of the mine? Morgan turned and caught up with the little parade. By now 40 people had joined it and walked along behind the priest in his robes.

Morgan rubbed his jaw thinking about it. An exorcism rite. He knew that the Catholic Church had such a service in one of its books. He'd never seen one done, never even heard of one being done. Would it work? Would it work even if there wasn't a real fire-breathing demon in that mine?

Morgan shook his head. It wouldn't hurt to go along and watch and see what happened.

It took them a half hour to walk out to the mine, and by then Morgan had talked with the priest. He'd never done the exorcism rite before. Ideally it should be done by two priests, but he could do both parts. He was a small man with spectacles and thin, bony hands, and the sharpest black eyes that Morgan had ever seen.

"If the demon can be exorcised out of the mine, I will do it," Father Rinaldi said. "It is within the power of our Lord Jesus Christ to throw out these lesser demons. We should have no trouble today."

"How will you know if the demon is gone or not?" Morgan asked.

"He will give us some sign of his anger when he leaves, perhaps try to injure one of our party or create some physical act of some kind."

When they neared the mine, the guard came out of his shack when he saw the group walking up.

"Afternoon, Father. What's this all about?"

"Yancy, I'm here to exorcise your demon. You don't have to do a thing. Is that the tunnel over there?"

"Sure is, Father. You want me to open the little door or the great big one?"

"The small door will be enough, my son. We'll stand just outside it and throw our voices with their power deep within the mine."

"Well, I reckon it's all right," the guard said.

The priest walked forward to the mine entrance, pushed back the man-sized door and held it open with a rock; then he shouted into the tunnel.

"Demon, Alkazack, I know you're in there. This is the power of almighty God speaking through me. We are going to cast you out into eternal darkness and damnation where you belong. You can leave now and save yourself the pain and agony of the ritual."

Father Rinaldi waited a moment and they heard nothing whatsoever from the tunnel.

He nodded to the two altar boys, who set their silver crosses down and from sacks they carried distributed small wooden crosses to everyone in the group. More people had followed and by the time they got to the mine there were nearly 100 people there, men, women and half a dozen small children.

When everyone had a cross, the priest turned to them.

"Keep this cross with you at all times during the next two days. Alkazack is a deadly demon, and while I will exorcise him from the tunnels, he might have some powers greater than mine, so he stays in the area. The cross will put fear into him and if he tries to touch you in any form, use the cross as a shield. Hold it out toward the demon. If he gets close enough, slash him with the cross and it will burn him like a flaming sword hitting the demon's form."

He paused a moment for everyone to realize how

important what he said was. Then he went on.

"I'll have to ask you to be absolutely quiet during this ritual. Also I want you to stay together. Don't worry about it getting dark. We'll be through and gone long before that time.

"Now quiet, please."

He turned to the tunnel entrance door and donned a special purple sash he took from his kit and then opened the smaller shiny book. Father Rinaldi began reading the ritual from the Roman Catholic ritual for exorcism.

"In the name of the Father and the Son and the Holy Ghost, let me be faithful to Thy will and send this demon back to the grave where he rightfully belongs. Amen."

The priest looked into the tunnel, but Morgan heard nothing and suspected the priest heard nothing as well. The priest continued reading from the ritual:

"O God, and Father of our Lord Jesus Christ, I call upon Thy Holy Name and humbly implore Thy mercy, that Thou wouldst vouchsafe to grant me help against this, and every unclean spirit, that vexes this Thy creature. Through the same Lord Jesus Christ."

There was a slight rumbling, but Morgan looked to the west and saw thunderheads rising. For a moment a jagged stab of lighting darted to a mountain top three or four miles away. The crowd made some oohing sounds, and the priest turned to silence them. He held the book with palms that had turned cold and clammy, but his face was serene and confident.

"I exorcise thee, most foul spirit, Alkazack, every coming in of the enemy, every apparition, every legion; in the name of our Lord Jesus Christ be rooted out, and put to flight from this creature of God. He commands thee, Who has bid thee be cast down from the highest heaven into the lower parts of the earth. He commands thee Alkazack, Who has commanded the seas, the winds and the storms. Hear therefore, and fear, Alkazack, thou injurer of the faith, thou enemy of the human race, thou procurer of death, thou destroyer of life, kindler of vices, seducer of men, betrayer of the nations, inciter of envy, origin of avarice, cause of discord, stirrer-up of troubles; Christ the Lord destroyest thy ways. Fear Him, Who was sacrificed in Isaac, Who was sold in Jospeh, was slain in the lamb, was crucified in man, thence was the triumpher over hell."

The moment the priest stopped speaking thunder rolled again, much closer this time. They didn't see the lightning strike before it but all knew it was closer. Dark clouds churned toward them now on the wings of the west wind.

The priest crossed himself, looked at the rolling thunderclouds and then made the sign of the cross at the tunnel entrance and continued reading from the ritual.

"Depart therefore in the name of the Father and the Son and the Holy Ghost; give place to the Holy Ghost, by this sign of the Holy Cross of Jesus Christ our Lord; Who with the Father and the same Holy Ghost, liveth and reigneth ever one God, world without end, Amen.

"Lord hear my prayer.

"And let my cry come unto Thee.

"The lord be with you.

"And with thy spirit."

The priest took both the silver crosses and stepped into the entrance of the tunnel and shouted the last part of the ritual.

"Oh, God, the creator and protector of the human

race, Who hast formed man in Thine own Image, look upon this mine and this town and all of your creatures here affected, who are grievously vexed with the wiles of this unclean spirit, whom the old adversary, the ancient enemy of the earth, encompasses with a horrible dread, that blinds and senses of the human understanding and threatens the life and limb of all these peoples. Here and now and forever more, expel and exorcise this demon Alkazack and cast him into the outer limits of hell forever and forever."

The lightning flashed the moment the priest concluded the rite. The bolt of fire daggered into a tall pine that had been spared the loggers ax. It stood less than a hundred feet from the mine. The 100-foot tree took the bolt of lightning in the top, split 20 feet down and both halves fell to the ground.

The roar of the thunderclap came right on top of the lightning bolt and the crowd lifted their hands to cover their ears as the thunder rumbled and rolled and then echoed down the canyon.

A moment later the first spatters of rain came down and the people began to move away from the mine and back toward town.

The priest gathered up his goods, put them in the small kit he carried and led his procession away from the mine. Morgan moved with them. They were less than 50 yards from the mine when a rumbling came, then a roar, and when Morgan looked up, he saw a landslide plummeting down the side of the mountain directly over the entrance to the mine.

"Run!" Morgan bellowed, and the people nearest the tunnel rushed down the trail toward the valley.

The roar of the landslide built and then the

first rocks came crashing down. Most of the slide missed the tunnel entrance, but half a dozen boulders three feet thick smashed into the small guard shack, blasting it down and pounding it into the ground. The watchman had run down the trail with the rest of the crowd.

In two minutes it was all over. Morgan stared at the mine property. Half of the mine entrance was covered with dirt and boulders. The large mine office had been smashed in on one end and dirt, sand and rocks piled up three feet on the crushed-in side.

Other than that there was little damage. Morgan urged the people to get back to town before they got drenched. The light sprinkle kept coming down.

When Morgan was sure that all of the people had left with the priest, he angled around the rock slide and began to climb his way up the mountain.

It was all too convenient. The thunder and lightning and rain would have come whether or not the exorcist ceremony took place. Morgan wondered about the landslide. In certain types of soil, such a slide would be easy to start.

As he made his way up the slope past mostly cut down timber, Morgan kept sniffing the air. He couldn't be sure. It took him a half hour to work up 300 feet on the side of the mountain. Then he cut over to where the first evidences of the slide showed.

Now the smell came stronger. It was like cordite, but not exactly the same. It was the smell that lingers after dynamite sticks are exploded. But there had been no roar, no sound of an explosion.

Morgan thought a moment, then nodded. Easy. Just bury the dynamite. It goes off with a thud and the earth moves and rocks roll and as the mass starts downhill, it picks up more speed, dislodges more dirt and rocks, and soon it's a full-scale landslide.

From here he could see the huge gouge that had been ripped down the side of the hill. It was 50 feet wide and had dug into the mountain 25 feet deep in some places, taking small trees, brush and cutover stumps with it.

The landslide had not been an act of God or of nature. It had all the marks of human hands trying to stop something, or trying to lessen the impact of what the priest had tried to do.

The sprinkle stopped. It was just a light shower. Morgan toured the start of the landslide and caught the strong smell of the exploded dynamite again. He looked for anything the perpetrators might have dropped, but found nothing. Even the shards of paper from the explosion would be gone, sent crashing downhill with the thousands of tons of dirt, tree stumps, brush and rubble.

Morgan knew he wouldn't find any evidence here to link the explosion and landslide to anyone. He'd have to look elsewhere.

It was nearly dark when Morgan walked back to Main Street. He was tired and hungry. Food first. He decided on the hotel dining room. He could go to his room to wash up and change his shirt.

He went in 212 cautiously, as he always did. No one was there. Morgan washed up quickly, picked up his spare guns and carpetbag from across the hall from Room 213 and put on a fresh brown shirt. He knotted a string tie around his throat and combed out his blondish brown hair.

Downstairs, Morgan went past the desk and saw a note in the box marked 212. He asked the desk clerk for it and saw it was sealed in an envelope. Morgan sat down on one of the upholstered chairs in the lobby and tore open the envelope.

Inside he found a note written in a small, delicate feminine hand.

"Mr. Morgan. I know you're in town about the Lady Luck mine. I have something valuable to tell you. Please meet me outside the General Store tonight at six-fifteen. This is all I can tell you now. My name is Gwen."

Morgan checked the Seth Thomas clock that ticked away on the wall over the main desk. It was ten minutes past six. He read the note again. No time for supper now.

Morgan left the hotel and moved down Main toward the General Store. The note had said "outside" the store. He remembered that there were no chairs out there or much place to stand or sit. The store had only a small entrance.

Gwen she said her name was. How would he know who Gwen was? If there was only one woman there, that would be a help. When he came to the store he found no one outside. The store was closed for the day. He peered inside, then leaned against the wall and waited.

He checked his Waterbury pocket watch. The cord on it had frayed over the months. He'd have to get a new one, maybe a piece of leather used to lace up boots. Strong, supple. The time was 20 after six.

Morgan hated to wait. He walked up and down in front of the store, then down past it one store to the alley. He hesitated before stepping off the boardwalk down to the alley surface, then did and walked across the 30 feet to the boardwalk on the other side.

Gwen had said the General Store. She might be there by now. Morgan started back across the alley when he heard something to his left in the blackness. His hand jerked his six-gun out of leather and he stepped into the darkness, watching ahead of him. There were clouds covering the nearly full moon tonight. He squinted, then moved, softly, deeper into the darkness.

A sound came again, a soft mewing, almost a sob. He hurried forward. It had to be a woman. He saw a darker form at the side of the building 30 feet into the alley. He kept his six-gun handy and bent over the form. A woman.

Morgan struck a match and quickly let it go out. It was a woman, her entire neck and chest were bathed in blood. Probably a slit throat. But she wasn't dead. A bungled job. He put his hand under her head and lifted it.

He heard the mewing sound again, faint almost a whisper. Then it became words. "Tell Morgan. . . . Tell Morgan that somebody . . . The mine, Lady Luck. Somebody is trying . . ."

The words ended. He felt her head and neck roll to the side; then a long gush of air came out of her lungs. Whoever it had been lying there was now dead. He eased her head to the ground and stood.

Morgan ran out of the alley and down the street toward the Sheriff's substation. This was something that Deputy Vaughn Thurston would have to deal with.

As he hurried to the office, he kept thinking about what the woman said: "Tell Morgan . . . Tell Morgan that somebody . . . The mine, Lady Luck. Somebody is trying . . ."

Morgan frowned as he opened the sheriff's door. How did she know his name? And who was she? Then the cold truth drifted down on him like a blanket of sea fog logic. She was near the General Store. She knew his name. The woman could be Gwen, who he was supposed to meet.

Deputy Thurston looked up from his dinner platter. He nodded in recognition. "Morgan, wondered when you would come around again."

"Deputy, I hate to spoil your supper, but somebody has just cut a woman's throat in the alley near the General Store. She died trying to tell me something. I have no idea who she is."

Chapter Seven

Deputy Sheriff Vaughn Thurston came to his feet, his supper forgotten. He reached for his hat, touched the six-gun in his leather and headed for the door. He picked up a pair of kerosene lanterns sitting near the door and gave one to Morgan.

"Dead, you say. Throat slit. Didn't die until after you found her?"

"Right. In the alley a door down from the General Store. I was going there to meet someone who was going to tell me something about the Lady Luck mine. She didn't show up. I walked around waiting . . ."

" . . . and you found this dying woman," the lawman filled in. "Not an easy story to believe, Morgan. I've been doing some checking on you. You've got quite a reputation around the state as a big-time problem solver, and not always on the right side of the law. Did you kill the woman?"

They had left the sheriff's office and marched

almost to the General Store by that time.

Morgan snorted. "Sure, I kill her, then come and tell you about it. You think I'm that crazy?"

"Never can tell, Morgan. I've seen all kinds of crazy."

They stopped at the end of the boardwalk and the men lit the lanterns, then moved into the alley. The yellow glow from the burning wicks soon picked up the form of the woman lying where Morgan had found her.

The deputy sheriff stared at the woman's face for a minute, then sat back on his heels in the dust of the alley.

"Be damned, that's Gwen, works as a hostess over at the Green Door Club, the best bordello in town."

"A whore?" Morgan scowled into the lamplight. "What would a whore have to tell me about the Lady Luck mine? She said my name. Tried to get a message to me."

"Then she was the one you were supposed to meet at the General Store?"

"All I know is the note said her name was Gwen. I'd guess this was the person. Somebody knew she was going to tell me something about that mine and silenced her."

A small crowd had gathered behind them. The deputy turned and spotted a man.

"Will, go get the undertaker. We have some business for him. Hurry along now."

Morgan stood. "Deputy, you need me for anything more?"

"Just a signed statement about finding the body and what she said before she died. Come around to the office tomorrow."

Morgan nodded. "Seems like I have a small errand to run." He walked past the gawkers to

Main, then turned down the opposite way to the Lady Luck mine and after two blocks, came to a house right on Main with a green door. A small sign over the door indicated this was the Green Door Club, the bordello where Gwen had worked.

Morgan went up the steps, past two brightly burning lanterns and through the green door.

As whorehouses went, this one was better than any he had ever seen. A wall had been removed to make one big room 30 feet across and half that deep. The floor had a hand-braided series of rugs, most round, some rectangles. The walls were bright pink with wallpaper and a lighter shade of pinkish white covered the ceiling. The ceiling paper came down 18 inches on the walls, and where the papers met a four-inch border of darker browns and magenta circled the room.

An upright piano reigned against one wall. A sprightly black man with white curly hair and formal wear with a bright red tie played whatever tune anyone requested.

Six men sat around in soft chairs and tipped drinks and ate what Morgan was sure was well-salted popcorn. He caught the delicious smell of food and he realized that the room looked more like a fancy dining room than a whorehouse. There were a dozen cozy tables set for two for dinner all around the room. The women in the room were fancifully and elegantly dressed, their hair combed and set in different and interesting ways. The soft music soothed the entire place.

Before he could see much more, a young woman walked up to him and smiled. She was a redhead with a delightfully low-cut dress much like many that he had seen at fancy society affairs.

"Yes, sir, what can we do for you tonight? Dinner, some drinks and some entertainment?"

Her smile was proper, her words even more so, and he found it again hard to remember that this was a whorehouse. In reality it must be an ultra-plush "parlor house" like those he had visited briefly in San Francisco one day during the course of his official business.

"I need to talk to the owner, manager, operator, whoever is in charge."

"Oh, is it about your choice of a hostess or something about business?"

"It's about Gwen."

"Oh, dear." The woman's face paled, her eyes flared and her mouth came open. She turned and scurried away through a door to the left. In less than a minute a blonde with streaks of gray that looked as if they had been deliberately painted in her long billowing hair came through the same door.

The woman was an elegant five feet two, with a sleek, trim body, well developed breasts and a tiny waist pulled in, Morgan was sure, by a whalebone corset.

Her dress and hair were immaculate. She appeared to be no more than 30 but he suspected she was closer to 50. She walked to him, nodded and when she spoke her voice was low and interesting.

"Please come with me where we can talk in private."

She led him through another door, down a carpeted hallway and into a room that was an efficient-looking office. A desk, two chairs, a file cabinet and a small stand with one of the new typewriters on it filled the ten-by-ten-foot room.

She indicated a chair for him to use and she sat behind the desk, looking entirely at home there.

"Now, what's this about Gwen? She is one of

our members and she hasn't been in since this afternoon. We miss her and are worried. She's never been gone like this before."

Morgan took out the note and showed it to the woman.

She read it and nodded. "Yes, that seems to be her handwriting. You're Lee Morgan, I've seen you around town. What is this all about?"

"Ma'am, I was hoping that you could tell me. Gwen was supposed to meet me, but she didn't show up. I found her in the alley near the General Store. I'm sorry to tell you this, but her throat had been slashed. She whispered a few words just before she died. She was trying to tell me something about the Lady Luck mine."

The woman frowned, then closed her eyes and lowered her face into her hands. She sobbed twice, then took some deep breaths and tried to compose herself. When she looked up, the damage control had worked remarkably. Only one errant tear remained on her cheek.

"Gwen is dead?"

"Yes, I'm sorry."

"She was one of my favorites. It's so hard to imagine. But I'm afraid I have no idea what Gwen might have wanted to tell you."

"Is there any way that you could check who her customers might have been during the past few days, or weeks?"

"Certainly. I can learn that exactly. The records are all confidential, as you can imagine, but if there is anything significant, I'll surely let you know."

"Ma'am . . ."

"My name is Charlotte. I'll investigate every man who might have any connection with the mine. I can think of none offhand who she might have gained some particular information from. Some men like to talk a lot, especially when they drink. We provide all the comforts and entertainments a man can wish for. Do you have any specific man you might be interested in learning about in conjunction with the mine?"

"Only one. Julio."

"Ah, yes, Julio. Not one of our favorite members. He has been denied admittance to the club as of last night."

"Had he been with Gwen?"

"I'll have to check that. Have you had your dinner?"

"No, I was . . ."

"Come with me. I'll show you one of our private dining rooms where you can have your dinner and a drink while I check my files and talk to some of the hostesses." She paused. "Would you like a hostess to keep you company?"

"Thanks, but not tonight. I'm more interested in finding out who killed Gwen and why. But I appreciate your asking."

"I want to find the same man. I'd be grateful if you would help me. Now, down this way. You can order anything on our menu. We do have the best food in town. For you it's complimentary."

She led him to a small room, no more than eight feet square. It contained a small table set with silverware and fine china for two, with crystal stemware and linen napkins. An intricate printed menu lay beside the plate.

She seated him at the table.

"Would you like to take your boots off and relax?" Morgan shook his head. "Why don't you look over the menu. I'll be back in a moment to take your selection."

Morgan checked the menu and was astounded. There was a choice of three entrees. Pheasant under glass, a complete dinner. Prime rib, a two-inch-thick slab of roast beef with a complete dinner. The third choice was a two-pound steak cooked to order with half a dozen side dishes. Wine and dessert were included.

The room had one small window but Morgan couldn't see through the luxurious draperies.

Charlotte came into the room a moment later. She smiled through her pain. "And what would the gentleman's pleasure be tonight for dinner?"

"The pheasant. How could anyone order anything else?"

She nodded. "It'll take about fifteen minutes to finish preparing. May I bring you a drink to help pass the time, and perhaps a copy of our latest *New York Times* newspaper?"

"Yes, the *Times* would be delightful and some rye whiskey and some branch water." He paused. "Miss Charlotte, I appreciate your helping me on this. Would it be convenient for you to share my dinner? I would expect nothing further."

She smiled. "Mr. Morgan, I would be delighted to share your dinner. Now let me turn in your order and see what I can learn about Gwen's recent clients."

Charlotte had barely left the room when a small Chinese girl came in with a tray and on it a pint bottle of Bitterdorf's rye whiskey, a decanter of water with ice floating in it, and a tall glass. She bowed low, put the tray on the table, then lay a folded newspaper beside it and backed out the door.

Morgan sat back in the soft chair at the table and poured some of the Bitterdorf's rye into the glass and tested it. He'd seen bar rye poured into an empty Bitterdorf's bottle. He sipped the whiskey and grinned. This was the real thing.

Morgan poured the glass three fingers deep and put in that much branch water and two of the shards of ice. It must not be river ice or an establishment like this wouldn't offer it as potable.

He sipped on the drink and tried to go over the whole tangled situation. The only way he would ever get Alexis back to San Francisco would be to prove that Julio was a rounder, or better, a criminal. Somebody had slit Gwen's throat. Killed her to stop her from talking to Morgan. It could have been Julio, or somebody else interested in the mine.

That was damn important, he knew. Morgan's one big problem now was who killed Gwen. His second problem was to find out what she knew that she didn't get to tell him. Whatever it was, it was important enough for someone to kill her to stop her talking.

Morgan spilled more of the rye whiskey into the glass and cut it with half that much branch water and another of the ice shards. The ice-cold whiskey somehow tasted different. He had that drink half gone when the door opened and a uniformed waiter brought in his dinner, pheasant under glass with all of the trimmings. He hadn't even opened the *Times* yet.

Behind the waiter came Charlotte. She wore an exquisite formal gown that swept the floor and exposed a three-inch crevice of cleavage. The tops of her breasts were pure white and showed not a blemish.

She smiled at him and waited for the servant to leave. When he had the dinner placed on the table and his rolling cart out the door, she closed it and locked it, then smiled again.

"I hate to eat alone, and you did ask me. Is it still all right?"

Morgan had stood the moment she came in the door. Now he hurried around the small table to hold the chair for her.

"I hoped that you hadn't forgotten my invitation."

He sat down and they talked little as they devoured the pheasant. He carved it and served her and ate his fill of the roasted bird and the thick gravy, mashed potatoes, and a host of side dishes.

"Dessert?" she asked when they had finished.

"Not a spot of room for it," Morgan said. He sipped his drink and held it up. "A taste of rye for you?"

She nodded. He poured her two fingers of rye in her glass and set the branch water beside it. She spooned out two of the shards of ice and put them in the glass, then downed half of the rye in one drink.

When Charlotte put the glass down, she stared at him with a touch of worry. "I have discovered several things that might interest you about Gwen and the Lady Luck mine."

"Please, anything that might help."

"Gwen had been seeing two young men. One was Julio. He uses only the one name and it causes us some problems. We have named him Julio X to keep him separate from another Julio. She had seen him the last two nights before tonight.

"The other man she saw worked for Julio. His name is Fernando. She told some of the other girls that Fernando was a constant talker when he drank. She wrote down what he said one night and was surprised. It had to do with Julio and his plans for the Lady Luck mine. She told the girls she burned up the notes she had made because she didn't want Julio to find out she knew."

"Did she tell the others what it was she learned?"

"No, only that Julio was delighted with the idea that there was a demon in the Lady Luck mine. He told Fernando they had to do everything they could to keep that idea alive."

Morgan took it all in. Julio was mixed up in the mine situation, right up to his eyebrows. But how did he prove it? If Julio or Fernando did kill Gwen, how did he prove that?

"Just now I heard from Gwen's best friend here that Gwen was so afraid that she couldn't work anymore. She was going to quit tonight. She was going to come into my office and say she had to quit and take the morning stage for Sacramento. It's too bad she didn't leave on the stage today."

Morgan stood and walked around. It seemed to help him think. He'd seen high-powered lawyers do that in a courtroom once. They looked like they could think better on their feet.

"Did she say anything else? Anything about the plans that Julio had for the Lady Luck? That must have been what she tried to tell me just as she died."

"The girls can remember nothing else. They all noticed how silent and frightened she was the last two days."

Charlotte finished her drink and stood. "Now, Mr. Morgan, I want to show you another room. It adjoins this one." She went to a drape, pulled it aside and opened a door. She went through it and held it for him.

Morgan stepped into a room that looked as if it had been decorated by the best designer on Park Avenue in New York. There were elegant pieces of furniture, lavish drapes, hangings on the wall, and an intricately handwoven oriental rug which covered the floor. Original oil paintings graced two of the walls. At the far side of the large room stood a four-poster bed with the covers turned down to show silk sheets.

"This, Mr. Morgan, is my bedroom. Only three men have ever been in here. One was my late husband, the second was the Earl of Dover, an English nobleman, and now you. It's been five years since the Earl was here. I hope you don't mind being third choice?"

Morgan watched her with a straight face. "Charlotte, what are you saying?"

She came toward him and reached up so she could pull his face down to hers. Charlotte kissed him. She pushed away and nodded.

"Oh yes. It's been a long time. Mr. Morgan, I'm asking you to be my special guest in my bed for the night."

Chapter Eight

Lee Buckskin Morgan watched the small, deliciously formed woman in front of him. He bent and kissed her lips gently, then pulled back so she was in focus.

"Charlotte, I'd consider sliding between those silk sheets with you to be a real pleasure. All of my other projects can wait until morning."

She caught his hand and led him to the bed.

"You're right, they are silk sheets. One of the few luxuries that I allow myself. Now, you'll be a second one." She trembled and he reached down and put his arm around her and pulled her close to him. Her blonde head nestled against his chest.

"I'm a little bit nervous, can you beat that? It's been so long I feel as shy as a virgin. Isn't that ridiculous?"

"Nothing unnatural or ridiculous about it. I'm a stranger to you and this is a lot more than just shaking hands and saying hello."

"It has to be for me. For a long time there . . ." She stopped. "Things used to be different. Then I got this place and I turned another corner in my life and nothing was back there behind me that I wanted. Then when I first saw you tonight, my heart beat a thousand times a minute. I could hardly walk, let alone concentrate on what you said."

"The wrong time to bring bad news."

"That, too. I've lost girls before, and I cried over every one of them. But somehow when you told me about Gwen, I couldn't cry. Maybe I didn't want you to see me crying." She pushed away from his chest and looked up.

"Would you . . . would you kiss me again?"

He did and at the same time picked her up in his arms and carried her the last few feet to the bed. The kiss ended and he lay her down on the bed and pushed up beside her.

"I've heard of you. Lee Buckskin Morgan is a legend in half the states and territories in the West. Some call you a detective who works only for big dollars. Some say you're a junior class honest-to-God saint who rights wrongs for the downtrodden who can't help themselves and never takes a penny for your efforts.

"My figure is that you're somewhere in between." She reached out and rubbed gently the swelling behind the buttons on his fly. "I can tell that you're not really a saint by the size of that growing dandy." She undid something on the front of her gorgeous dress and the bodice came open. She found his hand and put it on her bare breasts.

Charlotte gasped as their flesh touched; then she smiled and nodded. "Oh, yes, I remember the first man who ever touched me there. He was a boy really and I was so excited I scared him right out of my father's backyard. I bet he ran for a mile."

Morgan tilted her head back and kissed her again, then pulled her over so she lay on top of him and nibbled at her nose.

"Why is it I fall in love so easily, Charlotte?"

"Some men fall in love the minute a breast shows. That's because they're decent and honorable and don't want to act like a stud dog chasing a bitch in heat. For men like you it has to be a lovemaking, it has to come from an honest, even if temporary, love for the woman. That's the kind of a man you are, Lee Buckskin Morgan. Right this instant I think I'm more in love with you than I ever was with my husband."

She worked one hand between them and rubbed his crotch, found his erection and petted it through his town pants. She looked down at him, kissed his nose and smiled.

"When can I see him? It's been too damn long for me. I want to see him right now."

Morgan laced his hands behind his head and she slid off him. In a moment she had the buttons on his fly opened and her hand stole inside gently.

"Oh land sakes!" she said, her voice a little above a whisper as her hand grasped his shaft. "Oh, my!" She worked him out of the short underwear and soon he lifted through the pants.

"Just glorious!" She turned and kissed his lips, then moved down so she knelt beside his hips. Charlotte bent and kissed the long shaft, then held it and kissed the purple arrow head. One of Morgan's hands came down and caressed her bare breast.

"Oh, glory but it's been a long time. I wonder if I've forgotten how?" She giggled and shook her head. "No, I guess not. Like riding a bicycle, once you learn you remember."

She sat up.

"Lee Morgan, would you undress me? Do it slowly and let me know if you enjoy it."

Morgan removed her shoes first, then worked on the one-piece dress. He found snaps and buttons and when it was free he had her stand and pulled it slowly over her head, ducking his head under the hem and kissing his way up from her waist over one breast to her neck and then to her forehead.

When the dress came off her head and fell to the floor, Charlotte nodded. "Now that is the way to take off a dress."

She had nothing on except some French-style short panties which looked to be silk, Morgan decided. She sat on the bed and he went beside her fondling her breasts, watching her desire build.

"Yes, Morgan! It's great to have your hands on me. Such a long time, such a damn long time. Kiss them for me."

Morgan kissed her breasts, which had no sag to them, and now he decided that she was not much over 30 years old. He circled one breast with kisses, then jumped to the nipple on the other, nibbling at it, then biting it gently before he kissed his way around it and down over her flat little belly toward her mound under the panties.

"Oh, Lord!" She whispered. He moved lower, pushing the silken panties with his hand and planting the kisses until he came to her swatch of blonde fur hiding her treasure.

"Better stop, Morgan, or I won't even get to take them off. Stop and just hold me awhile. It's been so long since a man held me in his arms."

Morgan held her, with both of them lying on the bed. Her hand moved down to his crotch and toyed with his erection.

"Such a wonderful idea. Such a marvelous double-use organ. It's amazing when you think of it. You use it every day for nature's call, but then when prompted, he can grow ten times his size and get hard as a rod. Amazing."

Suddenly her hips humped against him and she turned on the bed and pushed him away so she could lay on her back. Then she pulled him over on top of her naked body.

"Please, Morgan. I want you to make love to me like it was my first time. Slow and gentle and like a real lover, not just a lover for the night."

Morgan's talented fingers worked their magic up and down her inner thighs until she was whispering and gasping for breath. He slid down the silk panties and tossed them aside, and saw that her legs had parted, her knees lifted.

"Yes, darling Morgan, right now. Please come in right now and let me dream of times long ago."

Morgan entered her slowly, then all the way and she wrapped her arms around him and sang a little song. She hummed and her hips began to grind around and back and forth and in spite of his resolve, Morgan became more and more excited.

He bent one hand between them and found the small note just below the furry swatch and twanged it sharply half a dozen times.

In the time it takes a lightning bolt to strike the ground, Charlotte roared into a surging, wailing climax. Her legs lifted over his back, her hips pounded again and again at him. Her voice wailed in higher and higher notes and then for just a moment she was silent.

Her whole body jolted and shivered with the spasms that tore through her. One after another they slammed into her small body, and she met them, and accepted them, moaning and wailing all the time. Sweat beaded her forehead and her upper lip. Her face distorted in a rapture of pain and then it was over.

Charlotte gave a long sigh and snuggled against him. She put her arms around him again, pulling him tightly against her body; now both her arms and legs trapped him.

For several minutes they lay that way; then she stirred and looked at him. "Isn't it about your turn?" She moved her hips against him then and growled and humped up at him and a second later he was thrusting at her suddenly in desperate need to have his moment of glory.

The realization of it came slowly. At last she lifted her legs upward until they sat on his shoulders and Morgan nodded and drove hard at her and when he bellowed in victory he exploded in a roaring ball of fire that raced around the universe and came back leaving him panting, his heart racing and his lungs starved for more and more air.

He collapsed and Charlotte laughed softly.

"Not bad for the first try. Next time it will be better and then better. About midnight we'll have a delightful snack the cook will bring up. It isn't often that I celebrate all night, but this has to be one of those times. Once every five years, I deserve this."

Morgan had two full hours of sleep when he awoke at 6:30 as usual, found his clothes and slipped out of the bedroom without waking up Charlotte. He helped the cook unlock the Mule Cafe and had the first cup of coffee when it came off the fire.

Morgan grinned when he thought about the night before. It would be a lovemaking he would be a long time forgetting. Even so, his problem was still at hand: to find out who had killed Gwen and what information they were protecting.

He thought about it through a big breakfast, then wandered out into the morning traffic as the town woke up and hundreds of men went to work in the shops, stores and mines, and a dozen wagons and small rigs jostled their way down the dusty street.

The mines. The Lady Luck mine. It all must come down to that. Julio was trying to get the mine, and he probably had his eye on the Grandma Wheeler fortune. Morgan guessed it must be 40 or 50 million dollars worth. Enough to make some plans, work out a scheme or two. But why the mine when he could marry the girl and get it all? Maybe if he married Alexis, Grandma Wheeler would cut her out of her will and leave her and Julio nothing. So, Julio puts off the marriage hoping the old girl would make a quick move to the closest graveyard.

Ah, true love.

So, Julio was the focus, but Morgan had nothing to go on. He walked down to the deputy sheriff's office and found him just waking up. Coffee helped him become human.

"Julio? I don't know much more about him now than I did when we talked a day or two ago."

"I think he was involved in Gwen's murder, but . . . I can't prove a thing."

"So why tell me?" the deputy demanded.

"Need some of your power."

"I don't have much influence in Hangtown."

"But you have the power. Noticed there's one bank. Want you to find out what the average balance is in Julio's bank account, if he has an account. The manager will refuse. You tell him it's a law enforcement matter. If he won't tell you,

you'll have to go to the county seat and get a judge to give you a court order forcing the banker to reveal the balance. He'll do it."

"I'll give it a try," the deputy said.

"Now, what about that detective who came up here and vanished? You have anything more on him?"

"Not much." The deputy got up and went to a file where he took out a folder and brought it back.

"His name is Nate Orlando. I've got a bag of his goods from the hotel. They complained after a week and I cleaned out his room and I'm holding it for him or for his next of kin."

"He check in with you?"

The deputy showed Morgan the form he had filled out for the impounded personal effects.

"Lord no, not a word. Some of them detectives don't like lawmen. Figure we'll get in their way."

"Nate Orlando. Good, I'll remember that. As for me, I'm heading back to the Lady Luck mine. Figure to do some investigating in there."

"Don't get burned up by that fire-breathing demon," the deputy said, and grinned.

"Don't aim to."

Morgan left the office and found the place where Karl Bullitt, the ex-foreman of the mine, lived. He had just finished a late breakfast.

"Karl, want to go take a look at the mine this morning?"

Bullitt squinted at Morgan. "Hell yes, I miss the old hole. What we going to do down in there?"

"Do some looking around. Want your opinion on a couple of things."

"Hey, glad to go. I've lined up ten men who will do what I tell them to. You said you might need some help one of these days."

"Good. Nothing definite yet, but I'm working on it. Let's get out to the mine."

They walked. It was quicker than going back through town to get horses. They found the guard in his usual spot. Bullitt grabbed Yancy, the guard, like he hadn't seen him in years.

"Yancy, you old roustabout," Bullitt said. "Looks like you're still here. Thought maybe that exorcism rite yesterday would do you and the devil in at the same time."

"Don't joke about the church, Bullitt. It was a serious affair and the lightning roared. To me it was the hand of God. I was down on my knees praying."

"Keep praying for us," Morgan said. "We're going into the mine. If we're not back in a couple of days, notify the sheriff."

Yancy's eyes went wide, then he chuckled. "You're fooling for sure. You not out of there in three hours, I'll bring in a whole troop of U.S. Army cavalry, horses and all, and drag you out."

They waved and moved over to the mine entrance. The piles of rock and dirt from yesterday's landslide had only half-blocked the small door which had been left open. Morgan explained the landslide to Bullitt, who nodded.

"Somebody out to keep the Lady Luck shut down," Bullitt said.

They went over the dirt and into the entrance to the Lady Luck mine.

"Should be some lanterns here where I left them," Bullitt said. He found them. They each took one. Bullitt lit his and they walked toward the shaft.

"Where would be the best place to hide a dead body in here, Bullitt?"

"A body? Like that other detective, Orlando?"

"Yeah."

"Down a shaft is the best place. But we don't have any that deep. Not the main shaft, which gets used all the time all the way to the bottom. That leaves the drifts, unused tunnels and some of the rooms where we hit a wide bunch of paydirt white quartz."

"Let's take a look on our way," Morgan said. They lit the other lantern and checked out all the drifts off the main tunnel. There was no place in any of them where a body could have been hidden.

They got to the main shaft and paused.

"Anything more down that way?" Morgan asked, pointing into the blackness of the continuation of the main tunnel.

"A dry hole. We didn't find anything back for two hundred yards so we gave up and went down. That's when we hit the good quartz."

"Let's check out the rest of this main tunnel," Morgan said. "That body has to be here somewhere."

An hour later they were back at the shaft with nothing to show for their searching.

Morgan leaned against an ore car sitting on the tracks that pointed to the entrance. He pushed away from it and snorted.

"Why not hide a body in plain sight? Somewhere that nobody would think to look. If they did find it, that would be after the mine started working again and it wouldn't matter."

Bullitt scowled. "Where the hell would that be?"

Morgan slapped the steel side of the ore car. It was almost four feet long and two feet wide, plenty of room.

"Right in here with enough dirt or ore to cover him."

Bullitt picked up a shovel from a rack and began digging out the worthless dirt and rocks in the ore car. He had gone down about a foot when he grunted.

"Felt something soft," he said.

Morgan held up the lantern and they both looked into the ore car. The unsmiling face of a man with a bullet hole through his left eye stared back at them.

Chapter Nine

Lee Morgan looked at the dead man in the ore car, then turned to Bullitt. "You know him?"

"Nope. He's not one from our crew, that's for damn sure. From the smell I'd say he's been there for some time."

"Agreed. That's part of our job done. He'll keep another few hours before we notify the deputy sheriff. Now let's go take a look at that demon at the end of the tunnel."

"You're serious. Good. About time somebody started talking sense about that damn demon. I'm anxious to see what we can find down there."

Bullitt hung the lantern bail on the crook of his arm and went down the main shaft on the ladder to the next level. Morgan followed him using the same lantern-carrying technique.

They walked down the level two main tunnel the same direction Morgan had taken before. Their footprints in the six months of mine dust that had fallen to the floor were obvious.

"You say there was some kind of an explosion down here, fire and all, when you were here before?" Bullitt asked.

"True. Man I was with panicked and threw his knife. It hit off some rocks, showered up some sparks and that caused the big bang."

They walked a ways farther. "I've heard of gasses that accumulate in mines. Ever have any in the Lady Luck?" Morgan asked.

"Not the kind that explode. That would have to be some kind of natural or methane gas."

"But neither of those types have been in this mine?"

"Not so far. That's why I wonder what could have blown up on you down here."

They tracked to the end of the tunnel, saw the burn marks and soot on the ceiling, the scattered digging tools, and at the end of the tunnel face, the six-inch-diameter hole.

Bullitt walked up to it and scowled. "So that's where the demon is supposed to have escaped," Bullitt said. "He don't seem to be mad at us right now. It's a pocket. We come on them now and then in mining. Some slabs of rock or gas or something formed a bubble when the mountain was forming or cooling and a million years later it shows up as an empty pocket."

"Bullitt, didn't we turn back toward the entry side of the mine when we came down this tunnel? How far would you say this pocket is from breaking through to the outside of the mountain?"

"Yeah, I see what you're saying. I'd figure not more than seventy-five, maybe a hundred feet."

"So this could have been a cave that once led to the outside."

Bullitt nodded. "Possible, just as good a way to explain the pocket as mine." He went to the face of the tunnel and with a pick, knocked out more of the thin wall between the tunnel and the pocket. When it was big enough to crawl through he stopped and held the lantern up in front of the hole.

Bullitt opened the glass lens on the lantern and put it in front of the hole.

"See the flame doesn't blow one way or the other. That proves that there's no exit out to the fresh air through the pocket. Otherwise we'd have a draft from in there into this tunnel."

Morgan took a length of quarter-inch rope from his belt and tied it to the bail of his lantern. Bullitt nodded.

"Yeah, best to take a look before we go dashing into that pocket. Hard telling what might be in there."

Morgan put his lantern through the hole and lowered it. He crowded forward and watched as the lantern's butter glow lighted an area that might not have had any light source for thousands of years.

The first thing he saw was the wall to the left. It showed as flat rock and when he swung the lantern that way he saw some kind of pictograph on the wall. Morgan swung the lantern again. Yes, some ancient people had painted with some kind of stain symbols and crude pictures. He made out a wolf and a deer-like creature.

"Take a look at this," Morgan said. Bullitt took the lantern and swung it where Morgan pointed.

"Be damned, then it is a cave that got sealed off and covered up. Wonder what else is in there?"

Morgan took the rope and lowered the lantern. He stopped well before it reached the floor, which he figured was ten feet below the level of the tunnel.

The end of the cavern he could see was 20 feet wide and grew wider as it faded into the darkness. Near this end Morgan saw a series of platforms that appeared to be made of stone held together with some kind of mud or mortar.

On each platform lay a human skeleton.

"An Indian burial cave," Morgan said. He moved back and let Bullitt take a look.

"Be damned," Bullitt said. "So where did the natural gas or the methane come from?"

"Say there are twenty or fifty bodies in there. The cave entrance became clogged and sealed. Those bodies decomposed, rotted and produced methane gas. That's what came swooshing through the breakthrough and frightened the miners."

"Dart Philbun would be afraid of his own rear end in a spring shower. What about that wolf dripping blood?"

"Imagination, fear, wanting to see something. Then when I came in here and Kinnelly threw his knife, the sparks ignited the methane that had become trapped in the end of the tunnel here."

Bullitt grinned in the pale yellow light. "Be damned and double dealt! That's great. Now we can get the mine back in production."

"Not quite. Most of the men believe the story about the demon. We have to disprove it or figure some way to reseal the pocket with the so-called demon inside."

"So the men think it's safe to come back underground," Bullitt said.

"You do much blasting in here?"

"Yeah, drill holes and blow them all the time. Damn hard rock, but no real danger of cave-ins. Notice not much shoring or square sets to hold up the top of the tunnel. Mostly solid rock."

"Good. When the right time comes, we'll blast down the end of this tunnel and tell them we've sealed up the demon again."

"When's the right time?"

"I don't know. Right now we better get back to the surface and bring out the deputy sheriff and the undertaker. Whoever that was up there in the ore cart deserves a decent burial."

Three hours later, it was taken care of. They rolled the ore cart out into the sunshine and helped get the body out. Even the undertaker grimaced when they had to lift the body out in pieces due to its decomposed state.

In his hotel room, Morgan had a bath to scrub off the stink of death, then had a late lunch. Helen Curley, whose father owned the hotel, came past his table.

"Is everything all right with your meal, sir?" she asked.

Morgan looked up and grinned. "It's getting better all the time, the service, I mean. Could you join me?"

He stood as she sat down in a chair right beside him. She lowered her voice so only he could hear.

"I missed you last night. I waited."

"Sorry, I got tied up in business." He noted that her white blouse was modestly buttoned to her throat. It couldn't hide her surging breasts.

"Going to be here tonight?"

"I hope so. Will you?"

"Unless I go crazy." She moved her hand under the table where no one could see and caressed the inside of his thigh. She leaned toward him and that let her reach all the way to his crotch.

"Oh, the poor baby has died. Just be sure to have him in his best stiff form tonight." She pulled her hand away and stood up. "I better get back to work or Pa will scold me again. Hope to see you tonight."

She stood, moved the chair into the right position, smiled at him and walked away.

Morgan did have plans for that evening. As soon as it was dark, he would visit the small office of Mountain Mining, where Julio must have his operation going. There might be something there that he could use as solid evidence of fraud or better, murder. The body of the man in the ore cart was identified by papers on him as Nate Orlando.

Curiously enough, Orlando had no wallet and his fingers held no rings. One bruised finger showed signs that a ring had been pulled off. It was something to watch for. It led Morgan to believe that Orlando had been murdered and then robbed as well.

A block down the crooked street, near the General Store, Julio sat in the back office of his new business throwing sharp pointed darts at a square of a cardboard box nailed to the wall. He aimed the darts at the bottom of a "V" that had been drawn on the target. Two darts hit half way up. A third dropped down an inch. The fourth hit so close to the bottom of the inside of the "V" that the pointed shaft touched both sides. The best shot possible.

"Yes!" Julio shouted. He looked back at his desk and the drawing there. It was a sketch of the mountain in back of the town.

He had been delighted with the exorcism yesterday. He would prove to the town that the rite didn't work, and that they needed him to get rid of the demon. Once he had done that, he would be able to raise enough money from the grateful mine owners so he could make an offer on the Lady Luck.

It was better than sitting around waiting for old lady Wheeler to die.

The lighting strike and the thunder yesterday had been a shocking surprise, but they worked remarkably well. His own added touch, the landslide, went off without a problem. No one could prove that it was started deliberately.

A nice touch, but what else? He had his big show planned for two nights from then. His man would be back from Sacramento tomorrow with the wagon of supplies. That had been a wise stroke. He couldn't risk buying the material here in town. Someone would have remembered.

For just a moment Julio thought about Gwen. It was too bad. He'd had many a fine night with her. Fernando had said too much and so it had to be.

He heard about the body being discovered in the mine, which brought him back to the detectives. The shot past Morgan that first day he was in town did nothing to slow him down. Morgan couldn't be scared off like the first one. It was time to take care of the man who had the balls to come right into the house and talk to Alexis.

The man could ruin everything.

Yes, Lee Morgan had to be eliminated so there would be no one to contest his sweep to power. He hated to use Fernando. The man had been pushed hard. Gwen had been a true favorite of his and the man was still angry about her death.

"May have to do the job myself," Julio whispered. Lately he had been talking out loud when he was alone. Did that mean he was losing his mind?

"Not at all," he said. "It only means I like to hear some intelligent conversation sometimes." Julio grinned. Then he began making a list. He loved to write out lists for jobs he had to do, people to see, small items he needed to buy. Now he made a list and headed it "The Detective."

How could he do the job? The man lived at the White Quartz Hotel. A shotgun and two rounds of double-aught buck into his bed tonight? Messy and unsure in the dark. He put it down.

A rifle shot from a roof as Morgan came out from the hotel in the morning? A quick kill shot to the chest, leave the rifle and slip down the back ladder and get lost in the early morning crowd. He noted that option.

Maybe lure him out of town with a note in his hotel box? Julio thought about that. He knew it had been used before and it had a certain amount of danger for him. Only this way he could pick the time and the place for the kill. No witnesses, no body, no trouble.

Julio grinned and knew he had found the method. Now all he had to do was pick the time to send the note. He'd get some woman to write the note for him. Yes! He'd say that it came from Alexis. It would have her name on it. Morgan would jump at the chance to help her. Probably wanted to get under her skirts any way he could. He'd seen the man stare at Alexis.

"Nobody is going to take her maidenhead but me," Julio said out loud. He liked the sound of his own voice. Yes, it would be a note supposedly from Alexis. She would say that she was angry at Julio because she had learned the truth about the mine. If Morgan could come and help her get away, she'd be ready for him to take her back to San Francisco to her grandmother.

Yes. Brilliant. He'd get Alexis out of the house so there would be no witnesses. The note would tell Morgan to come to the back door. It would be locked securely, double locked and barricaded, and Julio would be there with his knife, and with a sawed-off shotgun with two rounds of double aught buck. It would be like shooting ducks sitting on a pond. No sport, but tremendously productive.

Julio checked his pocket watch. The gold-filled timepiece on the end of his gold chain showed him it was past 5:15. He straightened the papers on his desk, turned out the light he had used and went out the front door, locking it behind him. Julio was looking forward to a good meal at the Miner's Restaurant, then a fine session with Ruthie, who would write the note for him and forget about it the first time he tumbled her in bed.

Ruthie was the daughter of the hardware store owner. She had a fine, chunky body, big breasts and was more than eager to go to bed with any man who asked her. She didn't realize she could be charging them. Ruthie was about a sandwich short of a full picnic, but she could read and write, and forget quickly. That was exactly the girl he needed, not another Gwen.

Julio walked down the street with a slight swagger to his step. In another week at the most he'd own a gold mine! Then he'd be a big man in town. Then they wouldn't dare to send him away when he went to the Green Door Club. Hell, he could buy the place if he wanted to. Julio chuckled just thinking about it.

Lee Buckskin Morgan watched from the other side of the street as Julio left his office and moved briskly along the boardwalk. With a casual stroll, Morgan followed the man for half a block and saw him turn in at the restaurant. Morgan crossed the street to watch the man be seated in the dining room.

Morgan figured he had an hour at least, maybe more if Julio didn't come back to his office. He walked down the street to the corner and turned up the alley that would take him behind Julio's office. He had memorized the storefronts so he could identify them from the back. He found the right spot and saw that the building was not as deep as most. It had one door in back with an old-fashioned long thin key lock.

Morgan took a set of three keys from his pocket and tried the first one in the lock. It didn't work. The second key went into the hole but wouldn't turn. The third key did the job after a little jiggling.

He stepped into the darkness of the building. Morgan struck a match to see his way, lit another of the long wooden matches from the first and found where the back room had two doors that evidently led into the two sections of the building that showed on Main street.

This lock was harder because it was different. He had no sample key. It did seem to be a simple lock with a horizontal shaft. He checked around the back room until he found a ten-inch-long screw-driver. Back at the door, he put the screwdriver in the space between the door and the jamb opposite the handle where the shaft should extend into the doorjamb.

After two tries he found it, felt the metal hit metal. Morgan took a chunk of two-by-four and hit the screwdriver a hard rap. The blade of the screwdriver hit the bevel on the locking shaft and forced it backward out of the doorjamb and the door swung open toward him.

Morgan stood by the open door, listening. The office was dark. He could see through the front windows to the street. He would have to be careful in showing any light. Then he saw the blinds. He walked soundlessly to the front and lowered the two blinds that would shield him from the street.

Just then he heard someone rattle the front door. Morgan crouched behind a desk, his six-gun in his fist, ready for anything.

Chapter Ten

Morgan huddled behind the desk in the Mountain Mining office listening to someone rattling the doorknob out front. Then he saw a figure step back and move past the shuttered windows. A flash of light from the saloon splashed across the man's face and Morgan recognized Deputy Sheriff Thurston. He must be out checking to be sure the doors were all locked.

Morgan wiped a bead of sweat off his upper lip and grinned. That would have been bad timing if Julio had opened the door and walked in.

Morgan used a burning match for light and looked around the office. It was mostly unused. Nothing in the files, only a few papers and scraps scattered on top of the desk. He looked at some of them. Lists. The man enjoyed making lists. One he found was for groceries and supplies to buy from the general store.

Another list showed the gold mines in the region.

There were thirteen of them. None of them Morgan had heard of before. To the far side he found another list that had the word "Detective" at the top. There were two entries. One said "Shotgun, 2 rounds, hotel room." The second entry just below that read: "Bushwhack coming out of hotel from across the street with rifle."

There was a round dot where the third entry had been started, but only the word "Send...." was written there. He scowled, looking back at the heading. Detective. Were these three ways to get rid of the detective? Get rid of Morgan? The tall man smiled. So he was a worry to Julio.

Julio would make it three killings instead of two; they could only hang him once. Morgan made a mental note to stay in Room 213 across the hall tonight and move around from now on. He'd come out the back door of the hotel just in case plan two won approval. He wondered what the third plan might be.

Morgan lit another match. He put the burned-out matches on a blank sheet of paper on the desk and would take it with him when he left so no trace of his visit could be found.

He had about given up the search, when he found another list of materials. Morgan checked it, hardly reading the items; then he frowned and started from the top:

"Four cases of 20% dynamite, 300 feet of burning fuse, two boxes of blasting caps, ten pounds of flash powder, two 50 pound kegs of black blasting powder."

The list made no sense. Why would Julio want all of that powder and dynamite? He didn't even own a mine. The ten pounds of flash powder was another puzzlement. That was what some photographers used these days to take pictures with. It exploded with an amazing white light. But how would Julio use it?

Morgan lit another match after burning his fingers, found the errant ember and put it on the paper. As he retrieved the match he saw another piece of paper on the floor. He picked it up. On it was the sketched outline of a mountain. There were mine locations noted at the far side, then nothing in the middle. The sketch had wavy lines through it in half a dozen places, some connected together. At three places there were circles colored in pencil dark. A mountain? Where was it? What did all of the lines mean? He put it back where he had found it and looked around once more. The match sputtered and went out in his fingers.

Morgan sensed more than heard someone at the front door. He dropped the burned match on the paper on the desk with the others, crushed it together, pushed it in his pants pocket and darted toward the back door. He had just slid through it and closed it when someone turned a key in the lock and pushed the front door open.

Morgan watched through a small crack between door and jamb as Julio lit a lamp and then a second one and placed both on his desk. He picked up a piece of paper and stared at it.

Julio chuckled. "Yes, my worrisome friend, you won't be bothering me much longer. Then watch out!"

Morgan crept without a sound to the rear door of the storage area, left the building and closed the door quiet as a whisper. Five minutes later he walked past the front windows of the Mountain Mining offices. The lamps were still lit and the blinds still down. Evidently Julio had not noticed them being up when he left and being down when he returned.

Morgan crossed the street and pushed a captain's chair up on its back legs and leaned against the wall of the store behind him. Just what the hell was Julio up to, and what did that listing of dynamite mean?

It did look like Julio was at least thinking about ways to kill Morgan. He snorted. Take a better man than Julio to do that task. But he would be careful about where he slept for the next few nights and who he slept with.

He wondered if Helen was in his room yet. He'd have to caution her to stay out of that one and use 213. Maybe he could get that one blocked off so they wouldn't rent it to anyone else.

As he watched the Mountain Mining office, a man came out, locked the door and walked down the street. Morgan let the chair down on its front legs gently and shadowed Julio down the street.

Yes, that seemed like his best strategy for right now. He'd follow Julio, see where he went, who he talked to, what he did. He'd probably find out where the man lived. If he did make a try on the hotel room, Morgan could stop it cold. It would be interesting to see what Julio did all night, and the next day.

Julio paused at the first saloon, passed it and turned in at the next one. Morgan pulled his hat down to shield his face, strolled in the drinking establishment and walked directly to the back tables in the darker areas of the saloon where the drinkers sat.

He saw Julio sitting in on a five-handed game of poker. The man would be there for a while. Morgan got himself a beer at the bar and went back to wait out the man he figured had to be a double killer.

Julio played poker for two hours. Morgan

couldn't tell if he won or lost. Morgan worked over his beers as long as he could, but was on his third one when Julio stood, cashed in his chips and left.

Morgan hurried out the door and saw Julio going down the boardwalk. He continued a block past most of the town's stores to a small place that sat by itself and had a small sign over the door. Julio knocked and waited. Soon the door opened and a slash of yellow light stabbed out into the night, then vanished when the door closed.

The building showed no lights to the street. When Morgan walked past it, he found out why. It had no windows. The faint sign over the door read: "Investments, Insurance, Land Office." Below the firm name was another one: J. B. Johnson, Prop.

Morgan scowled. Did this mean that Julio had a partner in this shenanigan about the mine and the demon? A partner in murder? Morgan turned around and walked back to the small store front office of the sheriff.

Deputy Sheriff Thurston sat at his desk playing a game of checkers with a bear of a man who looked up and smiled.

"Morgan, the big city detective. Solved my two murders for me yet?"

"Solved, just can't prove it," Morgan said.

"You're still hot on this Julio character? I admit I don't cotton to him but the judge demands that we bring him absolute proof."

Morgan sat in a chair and watched the game. "Oh, Julio did both of them. He's protecting himself. I figure by now he has worked out a half dozen ways to get rid of me. If I'm next, he did it."

The deputy look up. "This Julio threaten you?"

"No, not in words."

"You have met him?"

"Yes. Now to another subject. Is there anyone in town who knows anything about investments, especially gold mine investments?"

The deputy nodded. He took a home made cigarette from his mouth and pointed with it north. "Up the street a block or so, place called 'Investments and Insurance, or something like that. Guy's name is J. B. Johnson. Seems all right. Don't know how much he kens about mine property."

"But no problems with him. Upstanding citizen?"

"Kind of man you could trust your half-wild 15-year-old daughter with."

"Thanks. Oh, black has a must move there, a three jumper into the kingrow."

Deputy Thurston shot Morgan a barbed look. "Get out of here Morgan, let him find his own moves."

"I'll do that. Oh, any idea where Julio lives?"

Deputy Thurston shook his head. "Not the foggiest."

The other player looked up. "Hey, I know. He lives right across from me on Apple Street at Mrs. Hilton's boarding house. It's a big old house painted gray and blue. Can't miss it."

Morgan thanked them and left. He found the boarding house, made sure it was the right one by reading the small sign over the door, then found a place behind some shrubs on a vacant lot across the street where he could watch the front door and sat down and waited.

Twice Morgan struck matches, hiding the flame from the house, to read his watch. The second time it was ten minutes to twelve. Morgan decided to give Julio ten more minutes.

Five minutes later, a man who wore the same kind of jacket that Julio had on came up the street and went into the front door. It seemed to Morgan that Julio had staggered just a bit during the walk.

Morgan headed for the hotel. Nothing else he could do now. He went in the hotel by the back door, found nothing in his box and walked up the stairs to the second floor. Just to check, he unlocked his door, turned the knob and pushed the panel hard so it swung in and hit the wall.

Two lamps burned in Room 212. Helen sat on the bed, bare to the waist. A blush crowded up out of her throat.

"Hi, I got tired of waiting for you so I started alone."

"Sometimes it's best that way."

Five minutes later he had her bundled across the hall into Room 213, explaining to her his concern. Before leaving Room 212 he had stuffed a spare blanket and a pillow under the covers to make it look like a sleeping figure.

As she tore his clothes off, Helen said she understood his worry.

Morgan managed to get the door locked and the straight back chair under the handle by the time he was naked.

Helen lay on the bed, her knees coyly together, her arms spread out and her breasts still blushing.

"Damn, I'm glad you came. I was going wild."

"Wild isn't a good place to go, I've been there. You do understand why we moved over here?"

"Yeah, sure. Hey, I understand shotguns. Meanest weapon ever created. They're just terrible deadly."

"That's why I put the pillows under the blankets, so it looked like I was in the bed."

"Yeah, I understand that." Her eyes glinted with fire. "Hey, can I be on top? I love it on top of some big strong man like you."

A crashing, splintering sound penetrated to their room, and almost at once one, then two shattering shotgun blasts rocked the hotel.

Morgan jumped off the bed, grabbed his six-gun and pushed the door open an inch. He looked down the hall and saw a tall man with brown pants and a brown low-crowned Stetson racing down the steps and out of range.

"Damn!" Morgan said. "I'm in no condition to go chase him. That bastard tried to murder me. He would have cut you down, too, if we'd been in that bed together."

Helen had sat up when Morgan leaped from the bed, her face frozen with shock and fright. When she heard his comments about the shotgun, Helen gave a small cry of distress and fainted flat on her back on the bed.

It took Morgan fifteen minutes to revive her. She'd come to, groan a little, look at him and then faint again. He took a cloth and soaked it in cold water from the pitcher and pressed it against the back of her neck, then her forehead. Gradually she came awake again.

"Are they gone?"

"Yes. Nothing to worry about."

"We could be dead by now."

"Highly possible, except for this old trick of mine."

She struggled to sit up, almost passed out again but he held her. Helen giggled. "Damn, I don't have a stitch of clothes on my body. Ain't I awful?"

"I thought you were great, charming, and you had more fun than I did. You were fine."

She smiled. "Really think so? You're not saying that because I'm a cheap fuck?"

Morgan chuckled. "You must be feeling better."

"Yep. It's just that I ain't never almost been killed

before. It's old stuff to you, but wild and crazy and incredible to me." She grinned, her glance darting to the door and back to him. "Should we go over there and look at what's left of the bed?"

Morgan shook his head. "I heard the night clerk come racing up the stairs after he was sure the gunmen had left. He'll have a report on it for you tomorrow."

She watched him. "Hey, Morgan. I tell you about this Irish woman who had twelve kids? She was a little bit hard of hearing. When she went to bed at night with her husband, he'd say, 'Hey, you want to go to sleep or what?'

"He'd say it softly so she couldn't hear well and she'd say, 'What?' He'd say great and do her. Went on for years." Morgan roared with laughter and she grinned, reaching for his crotch.

Morgan looked at her. "Hey, pretty lady, you want to go to sleep or what?" He said it softly.

Helen giggled. "What?"

"Right thing to say, little lady, exactly the right thing to say."

By three A.M. they were both exhausted. Helen dropped off to sleep. Morgan thought back to the shotgunning. He couldn't swear there was more than one man on the hit. He only saw one man going down the steps and he wasn't waving a long-barreled shotgun. Maybe he used a sawed-off type. Maybe it was Julio after all. He'd let the deputy take care of it.

It would soon be morning. A few hours' sleep would be better than none at all.

Morgan awoke promptly at 6:30, but Helen was not beside him. She had left quietly, taking her clothes with her. He dressed, shaved in the cold water and put on all black: town pants, shirt and black leather vest.

This would be an action day. Black was harder to see. He had breakfast in the hotel dining room, left by the side door and before 7:30 he had found a spot on Main Street across from Mountain Mining where he would not be noticed by anyone in that office.

Just after 8:30 Julio arrived, unlocked the front door, went in and raised the shades. Nothing else happened until nearly noon. No one came in or went out the front door. The back door might have been active. Morgan had no way of knowing.

Yes he did. Karl Bullitt. He stood and hurried down the block to where Bullitt lived. Morgan hoped that he would be home.

They watched all afternoon and only one man, Fernando, went into the Mountain Mining office, and he used the front door. Morgan thanked Bullitt and sent him home. He had a quick supper while Julio ate his, then tracked the man again.

This time he went down the alley to the back of his store, unlocked the door and stood near it waiting.

Ten minutes later, Morgan heard a team coming and faded into the shadows of some boxes behind the store two down from Julio's. The team of horses pulled a wagon with low sides. In the rig were boxes and equipment all covered by a tarp.

Morgan moved up closer to watch. Julio brought out a lantern and they untied the tarp and began carrying things into the rear door. Morgan moved closer without a sound. The next box that came he identified easily, 20% dynamite, a case of it. There had been several cases taken in before. The wagon must contain all of the items that were on the list of explosives. Morgan scowled. He didn't have the slightest idea how the dynamite and black powder fit into Julio's plans to promote the demon and take over the Lady Luck mine, but he was going to find out.

Chapter Eleven

Lee Buckskin Morgan crouched in the darkness near the back door of the Mountain Mining office watching the last of the boxes carried into the lighted storage room. How did he find out what they would do with the explosives?

He worked it over as the men came out. One thanked the driver of the rig, paid him something and then he drove the wagon out of the alley.

The other man, who Morgan figured had to be Julio because his size, stared ahead a moment, looking up at the mountain behind the town. Morgan remembered it. There were several mines near it and the whole side of it had been stripped of any timber that was large enough to be used for shoring and bracing in the mines.

Julio went into the storage room a moment and came out again. He had a small pack on his back with shoulder straps and set off down the alley after locking the rear door.

Morgan followed him as silently as an early winter snowfall. Julio went to the end of the alley, then turned uphill directly toward the mountain behind town. It took Morgan a few minutes to track the man, but then it was obvious where he was going. He wore a light blue jacket for the night air, so it was easier to see him against the blackness of the night.

Morgan kept well behind him. Julio didn't try to be quiet. It didn't seem as if he were hiding from anyone. They climbed to a gentle slope of the hillside well above the town and Julio put down his pack and took out a few items. Morgan edged closer.

One of the items he had was a ball of string. A pair of small clouds blew away and the light from the half-moon came stronger. Morgan saw the man pound a small stake into the ground and tie the end of the string to it; then he moved across the face of the slope in what he must have considered a straight line. Every 20 or 30 feet he pounded in another stake and wrapped the string around it, then moved on.

Morgan couldn't follow him this time. Julio's pack was near the stake and the end of the string, so he'd be back. Morgan waited.

Fifteen minutes later, he saw the man moving across the face of the slope again; only this time he was coming at an angle to the line at the bottom. He was staking down the string again.

Curious. Morgan moved upward through light brush that concealed him to the spot he figured Julio would reach if he continued at the same angle. Julio came out a few feet below Morgan's estimation.

The man stopped and pegged the string to the mountain, then stared upward at the mountain.

He nodded and climbed higher, this time with the pack he had retrieved from the spot below where the string had started. He moved cautiously now until he was near the top of the cleared section. Beyond that a sharp cliff rose of bare rock and no growth at all.

Julio stared downward, nodding. Then he ran a line of the string straight down what must be the left side of whatever he was staking out on the mountain.

Morgan shadowed him in the trees, and once moving too quickly, stepped on a branch that snapped under his weight. In the darkness and night silence, the sound was jolting. Julio stopped his staking and turned, looking at the spot. When no more sounds came, he shrugged and went on with his lining.

Morgan found a safe place behind some light brush and sat down. He broke off a few branches so he could see through better, then watched the man working across the mountain. This time he took sight on the other side of the cleared section. Morgan figured the slash area on the mountain had to be at least 200 yards wide and about that same height.

What in the world was this crazy man doing? How did any of this have anything to do with the mine or the demon? It had something to do with that load of explosives. But who would worry about some dynamite going off on the side of the mountain?

A half hour later, Julio came back to his pack where he had left it in the center of the left-hand string line. He picked it up and started down the mountain.

Morgan followed him.

Julio went straight to his office, unlocked the

back door and vanished inside. Morgan groaned. He wasn't sure what he had seen tonight, but he'd figure it out eventually. Morgan was tired, dirty, hungry. One of the cafes was still open. He settled for a big bowl of stew heavy on potatoes and beef chunks and half a loaf of bread to soak up the juices. Then he hurried to his hotel room and checked for messages.

There were three envelopes in his key box. Two seemed to have the same hand. Upstairs in Room 213, he lit the lamp and opened one envelope. A square of paper fell out.

"Big One, I miss both of you. Can't get away tonight. How about tomorrow in the afternoon?" It was signed with a big capital "H" for Helen.

The second note in the same handwriting said about the same thing, only suggesting tomorrow night instead.

He looked at the third envelope. Maybe it could wait until morning. He was bone weary, not used to climbing up and down mountains.

He shrugged and opened the last envelope. In it was a perfumed piece of stationery with a printed drawing of lavender on it. The writing was softly feminine and precise.

"Mr. Morgan. I desperately need to see you. I've found out something about the mine that you must know. Grandmother must know. Can you meet me on Thursday? I can't risk seeing you in town. Please come a mile out of town on the Sacramento road. There's a rundown cabin out there where we can talk. Please don't let me down. I'll be there at ten A.M." The note was signed, "Alexis."

Morgan sniffed the paper and read the note again. The woman did sound like she was desperate. Some information about the mine? What could she know? Unless she had overheard something that Julio and Fernando had planned. If so, she was right, she couldn't risk meeting with him where they might be seen. Tomorrow would be Thursday.

The chance of an ambush brushed past his thoughts. It was always a chance. He had a way of reducing that chance to zero. He would be at the meeting place three hours earlier, in case there was something more to this than appeared in the note.

Before that, some sleep. Morgan made sure the door was locked; then he put the straight-backed chair under the handle. He would have his .45 in his right hand under his pillow.

He changed into his cleaned buckskins and settled down on the bed. He left his boots on. A man who slept in his clothes during times of danger would live many more days to sleep without them in a soft bed with an even softer woman.

Morgan slept like a newborn colt.

By seven A.M., Morgan had prepared his hiding place 50 feet from the rundown cabin a mile down the Sacramento road from Hangtown. He had inspected the fallen log structure. No one had been inside for many months. He found evidence of animals using the place as a shelter. A few pieces of furniture remained but most had been broken and stripped of any fabric.

Morgan left without a trace that he had been there and scouted out the best hiding place. The Sacramento road ran down a narrow valley angling for a pass in the mountains that would eventually down the hills into Sacramento.

That small valley a quarter of a mile off the main road had a baseball-field-sized meadow with pines and hardwood trees and brush of many kinds bor-

dering it. He settled down behind some four foot
pine trees with their thick branches. They formed
a perfect screen, yet one he could see through and
shoot through. Morgan had no protection from
enemy bullets, but decided he wouldn't need any.
He had brought his Spencer 7 shot carbine and a
supply of .52 caliber rounds.

Morgan had rented a horse from the livery but
had walked her in from the road through the brush
and trees, leaving the trail from the main road
unmarked. The animal was tied 200 yards away
down the main road so it wouldn't do any horse
talk with horses belonging to anyone who rode
in.

Morgan had no idea what to expect. The girl
might come riding up right on time, a little frightened and fearful. She might have important information or simply something she thought might be
important which wasn't.

On the other hand, a trio of sharpshooters might
show up and pick out firing positions to put anyone coming up to the cabin door in a murderous
and deadly crossfire.

He'd find out soon.

Morgan changed his position and leaned against
a sturdy pine with both feet out in front of him.
The Spencer lay across his legs. Heavy eyes closed
for a moment. Shafts of morning sun warmed him,
splotching his buckskins nicely to further conceal
him. He drifted into a light sleep only to wake up
a few moments later.

Morgan checked his Waterbury pocket watch. It
was a little before nine. If it were a trap, someone
would be showing up soon. Even as he thought it
Morgan heard hoofbeats coming down the road
toward him. They slowed, evidently to turn off,
then came forward at a slower and softer pace.

Walking now, he decided. The pair of horses nosed past the screening trees and angled toward the cabin.

"Around back," one of the men said. Both dismounted and one led the two horses behind the cabin and well into the protecting brush and pine trees. Morgan stared at the man heading for the cabin.

He wore a worn, low-crowned, wide-brimmed hat pulled down well. The man had the same build as Julio but even from that distance Morgan couldn't be sure. The other man had been Fernando, there was no doubt there.

Fernando came around the side of the cabin. Both looked at watches, then talked a moment. Each man carried a rifle, what looked like repeaters. The man with the low hat pointed out a spot to the left and one to the right of the cabin. Cross-fire positions. Fernando came to Morgan's side and about 100 feet from the cabin door. He vanished into the brush, and a moment later Morgan heard the man hacking with a knife or hatchet, and saw brush and branches move. He was cutting a field of fire toward the cabin door.

Morgan watched the other man vanish into the brush on the other side of the open space in front of the cabin about 75 feet from the door.

So, it was as he suspected, a kill trap. Morgan put the Spencer on a sling over his back, fisted his .45 and moved cautiously toward Fernando's position. The best way to eliminate crossfire was to do away with one of the riflemen.

It took Morgan ten minutes to move 20 feet. He angled into the brush and woods a little more, then looked around a pine tree. He could see the spot of brush he suspected as the hiding area for Fernando. He needed to move forward again.

Another ten minutes passed as Morgan crept on his hands and knees through the brush and leaf mold on the forest floor. He came to another two-foot pine and stopped behind it. Being careful not to show himself, Morgan stood behind the tree and looked at the place where he thought Fernando would be.

As he did, he heard a soft humming. The man was entertaining himself with a song! Morgan stared at the place again and now could see the brown pants legs of a man extending backward. He must be lying down on his stomach ready for a killing shot.

Morgan scowled. He had halfway hoped it was a real note from Alexis. He had no way of knowing her handwriting. Any woman could have written it. The scented stationary was a nice touch.

Morgan had another 20 feet to move if he wanted to handle Fernando quietly. Morgan adjusted the Spencer over his back, holstered his .45 and loosened the five inch blade in his boot scabbard. Then he squatted down and eased into the mass of trees, brush and weeds as he worked toward the bushwhacker.

Morgan checked his watch. It was a quarter of ten and he had moved into his favored position. He was eight feet behind Fernando, and still out of sight. There was a tree just ahead he would get to and stand up behind. Then in two rushing steps he could dive on the bushwhacker.

He'd decided on the quiet approach, a no-sound capture if possible; otherwise the second man would beat a fast retreat, or start firing. Morgan wanted them both alive and to charge them both with bushwhacking, conspiracy, attempted murder and anything else he could come up with.

The man lying on the leaf mulch reached over and scratched one arm, then lay his head on his arm.

Morgan ran ahead and pounced on the man. He had his fighting knife out and as he dropped on Fernando, he held the knife against the man's throat.

"One word, Fernando, and you'll bleed a bucketful and be deader than a headless chicken!"

Fernando nodded. Morgan eased back from him, shoved the rifle out of reach and relaxed his knife hand just a moment. It was what Fernando must have waited for. He bucked upward, throwing Morgan to the side. His hand darted for his holster and he had the weapon out of leather and halfway up to point at Morgan.

Morgan's countermove was reflex, automatic. He lunged forward with the knife, driving it deeply into the right side of Fernando's chest. The bushwhacker's eyes went wide, his gun hand faltered, then fell to his side, his body sagged and then dropped to the ground like a head shot steer. A gush of air whistled out of Fernando's lungs and his bladder voided, staining the front of his pants.

Morgan sagged where he sat on his heels. "Damn! You were a stupid fool, Fernando. No cause for you to be dead at all. I told you not to do it."

Morgan took a deep breath.

He checked his watch. Ten minutes after ten. He stared out the fire lane that Fernando had cut in the brush. No one coming to that front door would stand a chance of living more than a minute or two.

Morgan looked to the right where the other gunman should have been. He could see no disturbance in the brush. He checked it again. Was

it a little less dense at that point? The man had
been about 75 feet from the front door. Morgan
marked the spot, brought the Spencer around and
put three quick shots where he figured the other
man might be.

As soon as the third shot hammered into the
quietness of the high pine country, Morgan rolled
eight feet to the left and crouched behind the pine
tree he had used before.

There were no answering rounds from across
the way.

Morgan waited for what he figured was five minutes. Then he put three more rounds into the same
spot.

Nothing happened.

"You might as well come out of there. I've got
you in my sights now and there's no way to
escape." Morgan shouted the challenge, but again
only silence answered him.

He was about to move through the brush back to
the old cabin when he heard something crashing
through the woods. Then he saw a flash of brown
as a horse surged through a small open space and
jolted back into the brush that led to the main
road. He couldn't see who was riding the animal,
except that he had an old hat pulled down almost
to his eyes.

Morgan swore softly. He ran up to the cabin
and around back. It took him only a minute to
find the other horse. When he got it back to the
dead bushwhacker, he lifted the body and slung
it head down over the saddle. The horse skittered
sideways, but Morgan calmed her down.

He led the horse up to where he had tied his own
mount, then mounted and headed back to town.

A half hour later, Morgan was talking to the
deputy sheriff. He'd shown him the note and
described what happened.

"Don't you think that's stretching self-defense a little bit too far, Morgan?" Deputy Thurston growled.

"Hell no. This note is proof it was a kill trap. They came to bushwack me. They would have had me in a cross fire. And Fernando had his six-gun out of leather and almost trained on me before I stabbed him. It was a reflex, a defensive move."

Deputy Thurston swore softly. "Write out a report for me and put in everything. I'll see what the sheriff has to say about it. Now get that body down to the undertaker."

Morgan relaxed a little. The other killer was still around. "Yes, sir, Deputy, I sure will."

Morgan stepped to the boardwalk and started for the horse with its dead burden when someone marched out of a small crowd of gawkers.

"Mr. Morgan, I need to talk to you."

He looked up and found Alexis standing in front of him, a slightly puzzled and worried frown on her face.

Chapter Twelve

Morgan nodded at the young woman. "Yes, Miss. What is it that's bothering you?"

Alexis's face developed a frown. She pointed at the horse with the dead man hanging head down over the saddle.

"That's Fernando. People say you killed him."

"I'm afraid that's right. He was trying to kill me at the time and I beat him to it. I'm sorry if he was your friend." He told her about the ambush and she stared at him.

"Why would Fernando have anything to do with trying to kill you?" she asked, her feet planted apart, one fist on her hip, the other waggling a finger at him.

"I'm not sure, but I have some suspicions. I have to go down to the undertaker. Why don't I meet you in twenty minutes in the hotel dining room? We'll have coffee and I'll tell you everything I know about Fernando."

She hesitated. "Does this have anything to do with Julio?"

"I'll explain it all in twenty minutes. Please be there. Or you can walk down to the undertaker with me."

She frowned and stepped back. "No. No I'll meet you there. Twenty minutes."

Morgan nodded and stepped off the boardwalk, took the reins of the horse with its deadly burden and led it down the dirt-filled street toward the local digger man.

Half a dozen boys trailed along. One ran up beside him.

"Mister, is that really a dead man on your horse?"

"Afraid so."

"Wow! First dead body I ever saw. Can I touch him?"

"You should be respectful of the dead, not make a game of their death."

The boy hung back, then raced in and touched Fernando's shoulder and rushed away, shouting and leading his less brave band with him.

Morgan finished his business with the undertaker, turned in the dead man's mount at the livery and made it to the hotel dining room in fifteen minutes. Miss Alexis Wheeler sat at a window table, waiting. She looked up as he paused in front of the chair.

"May I sit down?"

She nodded. Her long raven hair hung down her back and framed her soft white face. Her dark eyes stared at him and wouldn't let go.

"Tell me about Fernando. I thought he was my friend."

"Fernando shot at me in an alley the first night I was here. He probably was only trying to scare me. Two nights ago someone blasted two rounds of shotgun fire into my bed in the hotel up on the second floor. I wasn't in the bed at the time, but a roll of blankets and pillows were.

"My guess is that it was Fernando. Why would he want to do such a thing? The only logical conclusion was that he did it because he was told to do it."

"If you say Julio told him to do it, I'll walk out of here. I won't stand for you slandering the man I love."

Morgan watched her and let worry lines etch into his forehead.

"Alexis. How long has your grandmother taken care of you?"

"Almost fourteen years."

"Has she ever done anything that she didn't think was the best for you as a person?"

Alexis took a long breath. She looked away and when she glanced back at Morgan she shook her head. "No, nothing that I can remember. Not until she said she didn't think Julio was the right man for me."

"How long have you known Julio?"

"For almost six months now. . . . I see what you're doing. But you must know that it doesn't take fourteen years to learn to love someone."

"That's true but fourteen years is a lot of love and trust and nurturing." He paused. It had to be done.

"Alexis, has Julio said he would marry you?"

"Yes, of course. That's why I came up here."

"Have you set a date for the nuptials?"

"No, not yet. Julio says we need to wait awhile. He has a big business deal he's working on."

"Does it seem strange that his marrying you should wait for some business deal?"

"Yes, at first, but he explained he's going to be terribly busy the next few weeks."

"I find that hard to believe, Alexis. If I were in love with you and wanted to marry you, I would let nothing short of the earth exploding stop the marriage.

"Alexis, I have to say this. You won't like it, but you need to hear it. I think Julio is putting off the marriage knowing that if you wed, your grandmother will disinherit you—leave you without a penny."

"I don't care about the money."

"I believe that Julio does."

Her face clouded with resentment and anger. She surged up from her chair. He put his hand on her arm. "You might as well hear the rest of it." She looked at him with anger and loathing, but settled back in the chair.

"I think Julio is stalling the marriage hoping that your grandmother might change her stance, or perhaps die. She is an old, old woman. I think in the meantime, he's doing all he can to somehow gain control of your grandmother's mine here, the Lady Luck."

"Oh, you're awful! I don't believe you can say such horrid things about Julio." She glared at him, pure hatred flowing from her sparking eyes.

"I also think that he and Fernando have been trying to get rid of me just as they did the other two detectives your grandmother sent up here to look over the mine problem.

"To cap it all, I think Julio murdered or hired someone to kill the detective we found in the mine, and the parlor-house girl Gwen. Gwen had written me a note saying she had something important to tell me about the Lady Luck mine.

"Julio was a . . . customer of Gwen's. So was

Fernando. I think Julio sent me the fake message yesterday supposedly from you, asking me to meet you out of town this morning. Then Julio and Fernando went early and set up an ambush. Their problem was that I went earlier than they did and was ready for the bushwhackers when they came.

"Now, I've told you all I know and all I suspect about Julio and Fernando. I'm sorry you had to hear it this way so hard and blunt, but I could figure out no other way to tell you."

Alexis had grown more and more pale as he recited the litany of his suspicions about Julio. She rose from the table, almost fell and steadied herself on the chair. Then she walked slowly out of the dining room. Morgan followed her. She went to the desk, registered and asked for a room on the first floor.

Morgan slipped away to the street. She was in shock. He hoped by hitting her hard with everything that she would think it all through and figure out that at least part of what he said about Julio must be true. Why else would he keep stringing her along about marriage?

It was past noon. Morgan ate a bowl of vegetable soup and had three cups of coffee as he pondered what to do next. Every time the plan came down to watching Julio. There was a chance that Julio was not the killer—that Fernando had done the shooting and the knife work.

However, in a place like Hangtown, an assassin could be hired for a few dollars in any of a dozen saloons. Morgan had to keep up his guard. He drifted down the boardwalk and went into the saddle shop across the street from Julio's Mountain Mining office. The blinds were up in Julio's place, but Morgan couldn't see if anyone was there.

He looked around the saddle shop. Here were

the best smells in the world. Morgan loved the tang of the leather. It was a heady sensation hard to describe. It made him want to try his hand at saddle making, the top of the leather crafter's art. He'd spent some time around the earthy, marvelous smell of tanned leather and it brought back fond memories.

The saddle maker looked up from his work. He had just done some tooling on the front jockey of an almost finished riding saddle. The front rigging straps were on and sewn in place. The latigo hung down almost to the bottom of the stirrup leather, and the skirt trailed solidly behind the seat.

"How long does it take you to turn out a fine saddle?" Morgan asked.

The man with the leather tool in his hand squinted. "You ain't a buyer, kin tell. Just a talker. For a talker I say I kin do her in a week. If'n you want to put down $50 for my best model, I'll take nigh on to a month to get her done right, with fancy leather tooling of course, and maybe one or two inlays of pure silver."

Morgan nodded. "Yeah, someday. Someday when I can settle down a little and count on keeping a fine saddle for a while. You see much of the guy across the street, Julio?"

The saddle maker spat a stream of tobacco juice at a spittoon six feet away, hit it dead center, and looked up. "You serious about him or just a talker?"

"Serious. I think he killed a man and a woman. Twice now he's tried to get me put in boot hill. Seen him around his office today?"

"He's been there." The saddle maker took a stitch with the beeswax-laced string. "You a lawman or such?"

"Detective or such. I'm trying to get the Lady Luck opened up. Way I see it, this Julio is one of the main reasons it's still closed."

"Don't say."

"Mind if I watch his place out your parlor window there for a spell?"

"Don't mind if'n it don't cost me nothing."

"Nary a round cent."

"Done."

Morgan wasted most of the afternoon in the saddle shop. He bought some new leather thongs for his boots and replaced the laces while he waited. Once Julio came out, Morgan tailed him. He went for a late lunch, then returned to his office.

A half hour before dark, Morgan walked down the alley in back of Mountain Mining's rear door. Halfway there he saw a small wagon loading something in the dusk. The goods came from Mountain Mining's back door. Morgan slipped as close as he could, and saw that much of what had been unloaded the previous night was not being put back in the wagon.

He followed it when it left the back door. The rig headed the same way Julio had walked the night before, and drove up toward the cleared spot on the mountain.

The team dragged the wagon up one last slope, then parked in back of the last house up the hill.

Two men struggled with the goods in the wagon. They carried them up the hill 30 yards into some screening brush. When the task was done, one man returned to the wagon and drove it away.

Morgan circled around and, using his best Indian stalking techniques, he moved as close to the stack of goods and the one man working over them as he could.

An occasional match flared to give the worker

light, and on the second strike Morgan identified
the man as Julio.

Now what?

Julio seemed to be measuring the black powder
out of a keg into gallon cans. When he had ten of
them filled, he picked up two and went up to a
familiar spot: the lowest end of the string he had
pegged down the night before.

Now Morgan understood some of the logic of
the move. The black powder would be spilled along
the string to make a powder trail. A match lit at
one end of it would burn along the path about as
fast as a man could walk, and it would give off a
smoky white light at night. Whatever pattern the
powder had been trailed in would soon show up
on the mountain as one large design in burning
powder.

There would be no explosion since the powder
was not confined and would burn quickly but not
explode. Not unless the powder trail crossed a
length of dynamite burning fuse. Then the fuse
would start to burn as the black powder sizzled and
crackled across it, to be followed at some measured
time later when the burning fuse hit the detonator
and the dynamite bomb.

It all went together now, but why? The scheme
was designed to do something, to promote the
demon? To give Julio some edge in trying to get
the mine opened? Morgan didn't know. What he
did understand was that on a setup like this there
were a lot of things that could go wrong. If the line
of black powder were cut, scraped away or covered
with dirt in just one place, it would cancel out all
of the flames and fireworks above it.

If one of the strings of powder was lit before
it should be, the whole effect could be quickly
ruined. Morgan sat back, laced his hands behind

his head and relaxed, watching Julio do all the work. When he was nearly through with it, Morgan would begin his campaign to disrupt and destroy the whole scheme.

What was the flash powder for? Some of it could be spotted along the line to go off in stages when the powder train came by. He didn't understand why all of this would be done.

It was nearly two hours later before Julio came running back to the cache of explosives and flash powder and fuses. He had been there a dozen times, now he seemed ready. Morgan slid around him in the darkness and moved out on the mountain 30 yards, and dug a trench two foot wide through the bottom line of the powder train. He moved straight up the mountain and cut the powder train wherever he found it.

When he looked down, he saw Julio standing and waving burning dynamite fuses. He held them as long as he could, then threw then down the hill where they wouldn't harm anything. The first three went off with thunderous roars, as a stick of dynamite will when exploded in the open.

Lights flared in houses below. A few men shouted wondering questions.

Julio threw six more of the dynamite sticks before he lit the trail of powder. The first dynamite blasts were a way to attract an audience, let them know something was happening. Then Julio stood back to watch the whole mountainside light up. Morgan ran to the side of the display, found a trail of powder and lit it with a match of his own.

The lower trail of powder hit a dynamite charge of at least ten sticks and a thunderous roar went up. A dozen feet beyond that explosion the trail of burning powder hit a square foot of flash powder and the brilliant gush of light turned night into day for half the town.

Morgan watched his own burning trail of powder race across fifty feet of mountain and then burn out. He ran higher, breaking the line of powder wherever he found it.

Below him on the mountain he heard a wail of protest as Julio had turned and saw the burning high above him where it shouldn't be yet. Then the line of fire on the base leg of his design burned out at Morgan's rupture.

Morgan saw Julio through the faint moonlight. He charged where the powder burned out and swore. There he lit another match and the line of fire burned again across the mountain.

Morgan ran across the slope of the mountain to the far side of the design and kicked apart four more lines of the fire. Below he heard another dynamite explosion. It must have been half a case this time.

The force of the explosion radiating out in a 360 degree pattern blew him sideways on the slope and he fell down. One more of the flash powder spots caught the flames and burst into a light blast that penetrated the night for a quarter of a mile.

Morgan turned away from it just as it began to go off and shut his eyes tightly. If he'd been looking at it he'd see one giant white spot in front of his eyes for five minutes.

When he scanned the diagram again, he found Julio running along the string he had laid. He set fire to the powder wherever it had burned out. He would complete the show, but it would now come to the watchers below in piecemeal, not as the daring demonstration he must have hoped to show.

Morgan jogged down the slope to the houses

of the town below and moved quickly to Main
Street. About 100 people stood on the boardwalk
watching the show.

"What the hell is it?" somebody asked.

"Who knows?"

"Must be that damn demon showing off his power," somebody else said.

The man next to him laughed.

Morgan got into the conversation. "Ain't no
damn demon, it's just that Julio guy up there
playing with black powder and dynamite and flash
powder."

"How the hell you know?" a voice croaked.

"I was up there watching him. Supposed to go
off all at the same time, a display sort of. It got
messed up some."

"Sure it ain't the demon?" the same gravelly voice
asked.

"As sure as I saw Julio lighting one hell of a lot
of matches to get that powder to burn."

"Them flashes," another voice said. "Ain't never
seen nothing like that before."

"Same stuff the photographers use to take them
flash pictures," someone else in the crowd said.
"Common, nothing miraculous about that stuff."

Morgan eased on down the street. Twice more
he put down the idea that the demon caused the
fireworks show on the mountain. By that time the
last of the powder trails had burned, and the last
dynamite blast had rattled the windows but not
broken any.

Morgan decided the show must be over. He had
no idea what time it must be. He headed back
to his room and saw by the big Seth Thomas in
the lobby that it was ten minutes past ten. Time
for some shut eye. No notes lay in his key box.
Upstairs he looked at Room 212. It was still his.

The hotel owner had put a new bed and mattress in the room and cleaned it up. He was just ready to turn away to Room 213 where all of his gear was when he saw a note thumbtacked to the Room 212 door.

He pulled it off. The dim light from the one lamp in the center of the hall was too faint to read the note by. Morgan used his key and slipped into Room 213 and closed the door. Inside it was dark. He struck a match and lit the lamp. No one lay on his bed. Good.

Morgan adjusted the wick in the coal oil lamp, then broke open the envelope and unfolded the piece of paper inside.

"Mr. Morgan. Perhaps there are a few grains of truth in what you told me today. I'm willing to have an open mind. I have been heartsick about Julio not wanting to marry me right away. That may be the key to the whole dreadful experience.

"If you're free tonight, please come see me in Room 115. I'll be reading until about eleven o'clock." It was signed Alexis.

Morgan lifted his brows, turned the light down and went out the door heading for the stairs. He wondered what Miss Alexis Wheeler might have to say.

Chapter Thirteen

Morgan knocked gently on the door of Room 115 and it opened almost immediately, as if Alexis had been standing there waiting for him.

She wore a proper print dress that he hadn't seen before. It was high at the neck and covered her arms to her wrists and fell to the floor. It did pinch in remarkably at the waist and stretched tight across the bosom to outline her full breasts.

She stared at him evenly from dark eyes as she held the door open a foot. "Mr. Morgan, it goes without saying that I trust you in my bedroom. You work for my grandmother and the smallest hint from me would have you fired and charged with any kind of crime I suggested to Grandmother. I want that out of the way first.

"Second, I'm still in shock and still angry from what you dumped on me today. You had no right to be so brutal, so honest, so damned right." She glared at him, then stepped back and opened the door.

"Please come in."

Morgan had left his hat in the room. His dark pants and shirt were still dusty from his mountain adventure. He knew he smelled of black powder and smoke, but there was no way to get around that now.

Alexis sniffed.

"You smell like a battlefield, Mr. Morgan. Where in the world have you been?"

He told her about the light show on the mountain and how he had foiled Julio in his latest try for power.

"Yes, I saw part of it. The flashes of light were dramatic. He did that with flash powder, the kind photographer's use?"

Morgan said that was the method.

She frowned, then motioned for him to sit in the straight backed chair and she stood by the window. It was open and the cool night air came in.

"Mr. Morgan, I've spent several hours hating you. I've also spent about the same time evaluating my relationship with Julio, judging it against what you told me, and trying to take a look at the whole situation from an unemotional view. That was impossible.

"I have decided that some of what you told me must be true. If that is the case, and I've about conceded that fact, then my relationship with Julio is not all I had hoped that it would be."

Morgan sat there listening. He nodded at the appropriate places but did not interrupt.

Alexis paced to the door and back to the window. "I'm still torn between conflicting emotions. Julio has pledged his undying love to me, has asked me to marry him, has been kind, thoughtful and patient with me. I have come to love Julio over the past six months. I thought we would be married by now.

"That is the stumbling block that keeps knocking me down time after time. If Julio is sincere, why aren't we married already?"

Her eyes snapped with angry fire. "The money. It's the damnable money. I can see that now. Julio used to tell me how poor he was as a child. How his family could barely afford to buy food for the table and they moved often so his father could find work.

"After a while, and after he had been to my grandmother's house, he stopped talking that way. Now I think it was that he saw the money my grandmother had. He knew that her money and power and position weren't important to me, so he didn't talk about it. But now I can remember how he *enjoyed* the things money could buy. He reveled in fine clothes, and expensive jewelry and a handsome coach and two that we often went riding in."

Morgan leaned back in the chair and crossed his boots on the floor in front of him. Alexis paced again.

"I'm not saying that Julio is interested only in my money." For a moment a brief flush pinked her neck and cheek. Then it faded. "But . . . there is a chance, I say a chance, that he is as excited about getting all of Grandmother's money as he is in having me as his wife.

"So since there is that possibility, what would he do to help himself gain that inheritance? I'm not sure. Put off his marriage to me? A strong probability, if not fact. I've wondered about that myself. But would he lie and cheat and even murder as you've suggested? Frankly, I don't know. I'm willing to have you prove it to me one way or the other."

She walked in front of Morgan. She had worked herself into an emotional state. Her eyes glistened with energy. Her breathing seemed to come a little fast, lifting her breasts delightfully. Her face had flushed with the emotion and she stood there, hands on her hips with feet spread in defiance, and she stared down at him.

"Mr. Morgan. That's what I'm saying. I'm willing to let Julio prove or disprove himself on the serious charges. If he's trying to marry me only for Grandmother's money, then that's a problem I can deal with myself."

She turned and closed her hands into fists, lifted them and struck twice at the air over her head. "Oh! I never thought I'd ever be thinking anything like this, let alone saying it."

She turned slowly. "Now for the rest of it. I'm sure Grandmother thinks that I'm sleeping with Julio. I'm not." She lifted her chin. "That was my decision. He left it up to me." She sighed. "You can tell Grandmother that. I'm not going to disgrace her before San Fancisco's high society nabobs by becoming pregnant out of wedlock."

She sat down on the bed as if her knees were about to give way. "There, I've said it. All of it. Well, almost all of it. What you need to know. I'll be staying here. I sent someone to clean out the house where I had been living. It's all here in this room now. I'll be here until this is over, one way or another."

She gave a long sigh. "Now, about the mine. Do you believe there is, or that there was, a demon unearthed in the mine?"

Morgan told her about the gas in the tunnel that exploded and about how they had determined that the breakthrough went into an old Indian burial cave that had produced methane gas.

"So you don't believe there ever was a demon in the Lady Luck?"

"I didn't say that. I just know what I found. For us it doesn't matter now if there is or was a demon; we have to counteract the public thinking on the subject. We have to convince those miners that it's safe to go underground or the Lady Luck will never reopen."

"Then you do believe there is a demon down there?"

Morgan laughed. "Didn't say that either. My job is to protect you and get the mine open. Julio's botched try on the side of the mountain just might have been a big boost in helping us win public opinion back about there being no risk in the Lady Luck."

"If you could pin the whole demon problem on Julio and then discredit him, that would be a big help, wouldn't it?" She asked him openly with no anger.

"It would. Only Julio was in San Francisco when the first demon attack came. But if he's using the demon idea to help get control of the mine, yes, nailing him on his miscues would go a long way to getting the mine open."

Alexis stood from the bed. Morgan came to his feet automatically.

"I win," she said. "I bet myself that you would leap to your feet the second I stood."

"Yes, Miss. Habit, I guess."

"Manners, Mr. Morgan, good manners and they are hard to find out here in the wild West sometimes." She smiled in a softly secret way and Morgan was intrigued.

"Another small bet I made myself, Mr. Morgan." She went to the door and held it open. He looked at her a moment, then lifted his brows and moved to her. Alexis stood on tiptoe and softly kissed his cheek. She stepped back.

"I bet myself I could do that and you wouldn't respond in any serious way."

Morgan grinned. "Reckon you're right again, Miss Alexis." When she grinned he caught her shoulders, pulled her forward and kissed her soft mouth with a lingering, just barely touching kiss that was strong enough to start his blood surging. He held her a moment longer than he had intended and then eased away and let go of her shoulders.

She staggered and almost fell. He caught her and held her against him, her breasts hard against his chest.

"Well now, Mr. Morgan. That's one bet I don't mind losing. I might as well lose it again." She put her hands around his neck and eased his face down to hers and kissed his lips once more, with the fire and heat that he had imagined lay just below her cool exterior.

She came away from his lips with her eyes still closed. Alexis gave a big sigh and then opened her eyes and lifted her brows. "Oh my!" she said softly. "This is one little detail I'm certainly not going to tell my grandmother."

Morgan smiled as she moved away from him. His hands fell to his sides. "You can bet I won't tell her either," Morgan said. He stepped past her and out the door. He waited until she closed it and turned the key in the lock.

Morgan stared at the door a moment, then walked back up to his room. He checked to be sure the hall was clear before he slipped into Room 213. The lamp was burning. He remembered he had left it on when he went to see Alexis. Morgan secured the room, undressed to his underwear and dropped on the covers.

He slept like a trail-weary steer until six-thirty A.M.

Morgan had a quick breakfast at the cafe down the street and headed for Karl Bullitt's place. The former mine foreman was finishing his own breakfast.

"Morgan. I heard about the fireworks on the mountain last night. You have a hand in that?"

"Had a hand in messing it up for Julio. He wanted one big display but I chopped up his lines of black powder. He's not a happy man this morning."

"He trying to prove something?"

"Probably was going to say the display was a sign from the demon. I corked that pretty well on the street. You busy this morning?"

"Not at all."

"Any dynamite out at the mine?"

"A bunch locked up in one of the storerooms. I can't get to it."

"We'll buy some at the general store. How much will it take to plug that end of the tunnel with the burial chamber?"

"Ten sticks should do it. But for that big a blow we better be a long way off."

"Ten minutes to get out of the mine?"

"Let's try it."

An hour later they walked up to the mine, said hello to the guard and went inside. They had no trouble getting to the end of the tunnel with the breakthrough into the cavern. They took one more look inside; then Bullitt planted the dynamite at a weak point along the wall where it would do the most damage ten feet from the end of the tunnel.

Morgan cut off 15 feet of fuse to give them plenty of time. The fuse was supposed to burn a foot a minute, but sometimes it went at twice that speed, sometimes half that speed.

"Ready?" Bullitt asked. He had just pushed the fuse into the detonator cap and pushed that into a hole in the bottom stick of dynamite.

"We going to blow it now?" Bullitt asked.

Morgan shook his head. "I just want it set up so we can blow it when we need to. I need to figure out some dramatic way we can use to prove that we've bottled up the demon in that same cave the people think that he escaped from."

"How can we do that?"

"Damned if I know. You get any ideas you let me know." They walked back out of the tunnel, up the ladder and through the main tunnel into the bright sunshine.

"How long would it take you to get the mine back in operation when this is all settled?" Morgan asked.

Bullitt scratched his head, then put his hat back on. "A week, maybe two depending how much things have fallen apart. Have to test all the cables, all the lifts the rolling stock, round up the men. Two weeks at the most."

"I hope you'll get the call soon."

They walked toward town along the trail that led through light brush and a few pines. Ahead of them a pair of California tufted quail lifted out of the brush and flew directly at the walkers. They saw the new danger and veered to the left into heavier timber.

Morgan stopped. What had flushed out the birds? Usually they would hunker down and not move unless they were almost stepped on.

"Down!" Morgan bellowed. He and Bullitt dove to the ground just as a shotgun blast ripped into the stillness of the woods. Hot lead whined over

their heads. They both rolled to the left into a
small dip in the ground just as the second barrel
thundered and more hot slugs ripped through the
ground where they had been and sang over their
heads in the shallow cover. They had been deadly
double aught buck, the .32 caliber balls in the
shotgun shells, capable of blowing a man in half.

"Stay here," Morgan commanded. He had his six-
gun out and sprinted for heavy cover to the left. He
figured he had ten seconds before the bushwhacker
could reload the scattergun. He made it into the
brush and larger pines, and smashed ahead toward
the gunman for 30 feet, then stopped still behind a
two-foot pine. He listened.

Ahead he heard a shotgun snap closed, probably
loaded now and ready for action. Then nothing.
No sounds came from the brush. Morgan waited
a minute, then another minute. He had learned
patience from the Indians. They could lie in the
desert sand for two hours, completely covered,
waiting for a lone rider to come near enough
to them so a brave could rise up and kill the
rider before he knew anyone was within miles
of him.

Now Morgan drew on that Indian training and
held his patience. A moment later a man cleared
his throat ahead. Morgan waited. A twig broke. A
branch switched back in place. The bushwhacker
was moving. Morgan monitored his direction.
Toward town.

Morgan figured the man was no more than 20
feet ahead of him and about that distance to the
left. Morgan leaped up and made as much noise as
he could as he charged through the brush straight
ahead so he would miss the man by 20 feet but get
to the north of him to cut off his escape back to
town.

He ran for 30 yards, then stopped and listened. He heard one cautious footstep, then another, and another. Each one fainter. The ambusher moved away from him. The man had been turned. Now he couldn't get into town and fade into the population. Morgan had him out here, alone, isolated, where he could run but he couldn't hide forever.

Now the work began. Now Lee Buckskin Morgan would track down this bushwhacker and find out once and for all exactly who he was.

Chapter Fourteen

Morgan had the shooter cut off from town. Now all he had to do was move up and take him. Easy to say. He listened again, heard more cautious footsteps moving away from him. Morgan walked forward through the brush and occasional pine tree, quietly making good time.

After 30 yards he stopped dry-bone still and listened again. The steps ahead of him continued, but a little faster now, with less caution. The man angled toward the south road to Sacramento. After listening twice more and then working ahead quickly, Morgan determined that he was now much closer to the target, not over 50 feet.

They were coming closer to the road. Morgan decided to gamble. He turned sharply and headed directly for the south road. Once there he could dart ahead quickly, estimate where the bush-whacker would hit the wagon-wide road, and be ready for him.

Morgan got to the road, ran down it 30 yards and paused behind a pine tree so he would be shielded from the killer if the man continued the direction he had been. Morgan waited five minutes, then heard someone coming. He was on the near side of Morgan, so the detective slid around the big pine so it would shield him.

The sounds of footsteps came louder now, the man not trying for silence, seemingly rushing for the road. Morgan cocked his six-gun holding the hammer so it would make as little noise as possible.

The man burst out of some brush 20 feet up the road, the shotgun at port arms, sweat dripping from his red face. The man was Julio.

Morgan leaned around the pine. "Hold it, Julio. You move a muscle and you're dead."

Julio never paused in his step, the shotgun jolted down a foot and he blasted a round at the sound of the voice. Morgan got off a shot before he lunged behind the pine tree. The two shots came almost together, the heavier, authoritative blast of the 10-gauge shotgun and the more strident bark of the .45.

Morgan heard the double-aught buck rounds slam into the pine, felt the breeze of some of the slugs that just missed the tree and slashed past into the brush.

Julio had two shots, Morgan had four more. He peered out on the opposite side of the tree and saw Julio fire again. This time Morgan dropped to the ground behind the tree, chanced a look around the right side of the tree and snapped off another round.

He felt the double-aught buck rounds hit the tree up high and others miss on the far side. His own round struck home, but the snap shot produced only a shoulder wound. Julio screamed as the bullet hit him, driving him back into the brush at the side of the road.

Morgan had lost his target. He could rush the man before he could reload. Then Morgan remembered the six-gun in leather at Julio's hip. He couldn't rush a hogleg. Morgan darted away from the pine into the brush that still concealed Julio. The brush moved ahead of him; then he sensed more than heard Julio leaving.

There were a few telltale signs, then positive evidence as Morgan heard Julio running through the brush back the way he had come, toward the Lady Luck mine. Julio might have some resources there, or some confederates.

Morgan paced the sounds in front of him. Yes, the man was heading for the mine. It was up a small valley and toward a ridge that thrust upward dramatically with a barren slab of granite on the very top.

Morgan ran faster to close the gap. As he ran he kicked out the spent two rounds and loaded in three more so he had six bullets in his weapon. He left the hammer down gently. Any serious jolt of the Colt could bounce the hammer back far enough to cause it to fire when it fell back forward. He'd be careful.

Morgan came to the edge of the clearing around the Lady Luck mine and spotted Julio in his gray jacket darting around the guard shack and running into the Lady Luck tunnel entrance. Why was he going in there?

Morgan rushed from cover to cover. Julio had a perfect fortress to hold off half an army if he chose to use it. He could hide just inside behind the heavy plank door and pick off anyone trying to get to the entrance.

Morgan held his hat out from behind the guard shack door, but took no fire.

"What in tarnation is going on?" the guard bleated.

"We've got a trespasser in the mine. I'm going in after him."

Morgan darted ahead toward the door, firing one shot through the opening to keep any head down. He got to the entrance beside the door without taking any fire. Again he held his hat out, this time in front of the open door. Nothing happened. Morgan jammed his hat back on and ran at an angle through the door, then dropped to the tunnel floor.

He was inside, but still hadn't made contact with Julio. He closed his eyes a minute, then turned and stared down the dark tunnel. Far down he could see a gently bobbing light. Someone was moving into the mine with a lighted lantern.

Morgan found the lantern he had left near the opening, lit it and hurried after Julio. He had no idea why the man was in there.

There were too many tracks down the tunnel in the dust for him to be able to follow Julio's prints. Morgan moved ahead swiftly, hoping to overtake the man.

He came to the main shaft and had not run into Julio. Would he have gone down the shaft? He must know where the tunnel was with the Indian cave. Why would he go there?

Morgan hung the bail of his lantern over his arm and went down the wooden ladder one level to the tunnel and looked down toward the Indian cave. He saw the moving lantern, much closer this time.

"Julio, give it up. You don't have a chance down here. Maybe the demon will get you."

He heard nothing in response but a caustic laugh. Morgan logged ahead through the tunnel. It was eight feet high here and the rails fixed in ties buried in the floor. Morgan couldn't figure Julio. Why was he down here?

He tried again. "Julio, you're a smart man. Why are you down here? You can't prove anything here. You won't scare me with any demon stories and kill me the way you did that other detective."

Julio only laughed.

Morgan worked his way down the tunnel. He was about 100 feet from the end of it now. He could see the light from the lantern playing on the tools abandoned there by the miners.

Morgan saw the lantern held higher, evidently when Julio investigated the breakthrough into the cave. Then the light vanished. He probably had pushed it into the Indian burial cave to look at it.

Morgan worked forward until he was within 50 feet of the end of the tunnel. Julio had pulled the lantern out of the cavern and stood at the end of the tunnel. He had the shotgun but pointed it at the ground.

In the faint glow of the lantern ten feet from the end of the cave, Morgan could see the pile of rocks Bullitt had shoveled over the dynamite bomb. The black burning fuse that ran away from it blended into the dirt on the floor.

Morgan hoped that Julio didn't notice it. Morgan could tell about where the end of the 15-foot fuse lay.

"Julio, let's talk. No sense in killing each other down here. Let's get it out in the open and work out a solution."

"Ain't no solution. You turned my girl against me."

"She wasn't yours or you would have married her two months ago. You were afraid of losing the inheritance."

"Damn you, Morgan!" He lifted the shotgun and pulled the trigger. Morgan dove to the left into a small niche. This was one of many spots in the tunnels where the boys who ran dynamite from the main supply to the tunnel face crawled to so they wouldn't be blasted back down the tunnel by the dynamite explosion.

Morgan curled into it just in time but felt one heavy double-aught buck slug glance off the heel of his boot.

The detonation of the shotgun in the tunnel sounded ten times as loud as usual because of the confined space. The sound rolled down the tunnel and bounced back from the far end.

Morgan peered out of the hole. Dirt and small rocks filtered down from the ceiling. Smoke and dust filled the air until he couldn't see plainly.

"Morgan, you still alive?"

Morgan didn't answer. "Yeah, figured not. About time I take a look in that damn grave cave to find the gold. Some of the Indians buried themselves with heavy chunks of pure gold."

As the dust settled, Morgan could see the end of the tunnel in bits and pieces. When the last of the dust fell, Morgan couldn't find Julio anywhere.

The light from Julio's lantern didn't show at the end of the tunnel. Morgan moved forward cautiously, his lantern in hand. He knew he made a perfect target but there was no other way to find Julio.

He crept up to the breakthrough at the end of the tunnel. Inside he saw the light from a lantern. Then he saw Julio among the stone tables and the raw skeletons.

"Julio, get out of there. That's a cemetery, a graveyard."

"Shut up, Morgan. I came to find the buried gold and I'm gonna find it. It's in here. Know damn well it's here. All these Indians up in here buried their chiefs with gold. Pounds and pounds of gold. I've head the stories."

"Not true, Julio. Get out of there."

Julio lifted the shotgun and fired. Morgan saw the weapon coming up and ducked to the floor behind the solid part of the rock wall. The heavy slugs drilled more rock and stone from the hole through the wall but missed Morgan.

The sound was muffled by the cave and only part of the sound came though the small breakthrough hole. Then Morgan heard another sound. A rumbling; earth moving. He lifted up and looked in the hole. The lantern light had gone out.

"Julio, where are you?" Morgan called.

A faint cry came back; then it grew stronger. "In here. Come and get me, Morgan. You can't leave me in here with all these dead Indians."

"I can't see you."

"Part of the roof caved in. From the shot I guess. My legs are trapped. Come get me, damn it!"

Morgan pushed the lantern through the hole and let the light filter through the still settling dust of the cave in. A moment later it cleared and he spotted Julio 20 feet from the end of the cave. A great pile of dirt and rocks covered most of him. Only his head, shoulders and one arm showed above the rocks and dirt.

"I'll get you," Morgan said. "Tell me. Did you kill that detective, Nate Orlando?"

"Yeah. I had to. Now come get me. Orlando was getting too nosy. Hurry up some more of this ceiling might fall."

"I'll get a shovel." Morgan pulled the lantern back through the hole and found a shovel nearby. He dropped it through the hole, then pushed the lantern back through.

"Thank God, you came back!" Julio wailed.

"What about Gwen, the parlor house girl. You use your knife on her?"

"Gwen? Nice little woman. But she talked too much. I had to keep her quiet. Had to. Now get in here!"

Morgan eyed the ten-foot drop to the bottom of the Indian burial cave. He could do it, but could he get back out? Maybe pile up enough rocks to jump up and get hold of the hole. Yes, it could be done. Tie a rope on the lantern and let it down. Use the rope to pull himself back up. Yes.

He had tied the lantern to the rope and let it down, just as the roof of the cavern rumbled again and a few rocks fell.

"Hurry up, damn it. I'm getting more cave-in over here."

Morgan tried to look at the top of the cave but it was up too far. He tied off the half-inch rope to the middle of a shovel. It would pull up and form a bar across the hole so he could use the anchored rope to climb back out.

He pushed his legs through the hole and moved down farther. Morgan was just about ready to drop to the bottom of the cave when he heard the earth rumbling around him.

Julio screamed. "Damn, it's coming again. Hurry up!"

Morgan couldn't see what went on in the cavern. His head was still in the tunnel. He pulled himself out of the hole, got his feet on the tunnel floor and looked back into the cave. Dirt and rocks sifted down on Julio. He could see the man's head.

Julio screamed again. Then a heavy fall came crashing down and Julio's screams muffled to silence.

After two or three minutes the fall stopped. Morgan swung the lantern out wide so he could see better. The spot where he last saw Julio was buried under ten feet of rocks and dirt. There was no reason to try to save him now. Julio had to be dead already under all of that dirt and rock.

Morgan pulled the lantern up and through the hole, then sat down and leaned against the back of the tunnel. Julio was dead and gone. Retribution for his own dirty deeds? One score settled.

What about the demon?

Morgan stood and walked slowly down the tunnel away from the end. The answer he'd been trying for came and he nodded, picked up his pace and found the length of dynamite fuse. He followed it back to the bomb, pawed away the dirt and rocks to be sure nothing would snuff out the fuse all the way to the detonator.

Then he followed the fuse back to the end. It didn't seem like a lot of time. Fifteen feet should be 15 minutes. He hoped he hadn't bought a batch of "fast" fuse. Morgan took a match out of his pocket and stared at it a moment. Then he held it over the vent in the lantern and the match burst into flames. He touched it to the end of the burn fuse, made certain it was on fire and sputtering; then he turned and ran.

It took what Morgan figured was five minutes to run out of the mine. He stood outside panting and waiting.

After what he guessed were the longest ten minutes in his life, the dynamite went off deep in the mine. He felt only a slight shudder of the earth, and then several minutes later a weak plume of dust and smoke gushed out of the entrance to the Lady Luck gold mine.

The guard came running up. "What the hell's that smoke?"

"What smoke?" Morgan asked. "You seeing the demon again?"

"Oh, no, not me. Ain't no demon. I know that. Most of us know that. Just something different for a change. A little wild story that got out of hand. Just a little excitement."

Morgan waited an hour for the dust to settle in the dynamited tunnel, then took the old guard with him into the mine to verify what he found.

The dynamite had collapsed the tunnel for 15 feet and completely sealed off the tunnel and the Indian burial cave.

"See that, old timer?" Morgan asked. "That explosion walls off the demon, keeps him trapped back there in that cave where he lived. He never will be able to get out again. I want you to be sure to tell everyone you see that the demon of the Lady Luck mine is forever sealed up again in his tomb."

"Glory be, I can do that. Hell, yes, I can do that!"

Morgan chuckled at the old man's enthusiasm. "You stay here for now. I've got to get back into town and start arrangements to get the Lady Luck back into operation."

Chapter Fifteen

That evening, Lee Morgan made a complete written statement for the deputy sheriff. He swore that Julio had confessed to killing the detective, Nate Orlando, dumping him in the ore car and covering him with dirt and rocks. Julio also confessed that he killed Gwen with a knife.

Morgan spelled out what happened in the burial cave and told how the shotgun blast had loosened the rock fall from the ceiling that killed the murderer.

"Then the guard on the mine, Old Yancy, returned to the tunnel with me and we inspected the damage the dynamite blast I set off had done. It collapsed the far end of the tunnel, completely blocking off the tunnel about ten feet from the breakthrough, and thereby sealing in the old Indian burial cave forever."

Morgan added what more facts he figured would be needed, then signed the document and gave it to the deputy.

"This it?" Deputy Sheriff Thurston asked.

"Figure as how. Be around for another day or so if'n you have any questions."

"Man died out there, Morgan. Bound to be a lot of questions."

"I just answered them all."

He ducked out and headed for the hotel. By the time he got there he knew that the story was all over town. He spotted Karl Bullitt, the former foreman from the Lady Luck mine. He was talking to a crowd of men outside a saloon. Bullitt saw Morgan and waved him over.

"Just telling the men that the demon, if there was one, has been sealed in the end of the tunnel, and we'll work around that section searching for more white quartz. I figured we'd start getting the mine back in shape tomorrow morning, if it's all right with you."

"I can authorize it," Morgan said. "Get me a list of the men you'll need and what equipment and how long you'll need to get the mine ready for full production."

Bullitt grinned and pumped Morgan's hand. "Yes sir! We can do that. Have a list for you first thing in the morning at the front desk of the White Quartz Hotel." He rushed off to talk to the crowd of men and before Morgan was out of earshot, he heard a shout go up and then cheering.

He'd get a telegram off by stage in the morning to be sent from Sacramento asking for permission to reopen the mine. He felt Mrs. Wheeler would approve. She'd also have to reopen bank accounts in Hangtown, bring in a general manager and take care of a few other details.

In the meantime, Morgan wanted to stretch out on a soft bed and have a rest.

He went in the hotel and checked his key box. Three messages. Two of them from Helen Curley, the sexy daughter of the hotel owner. The third in a woman's hand he didn't recognize. He read that one.

"Mr. Morgan. I just heard about the story at the mine. Hope it's true. Then the mine can reopen and grandmother will be pleased. I'd like to speak with you unless you get in too late. I'll be reading until at least eleven tonight." It was signed with a big fancy "A".

He put the notes in his pocket and hurried up to Room 213. Morgan used caution going inside as usual. No one was there. He washed his hands and face and torso in a bowl of cold water provided and dried himself. Then he slipped on clean town pants and a soft brown shirt and his brown leather vest. His boots needed polish, but then they always did.

Morgan combed his hair best he could and slapped some rose water and bay rum on his face. When he looked in the wavy mirror over the dresser he decided that was the best he could do.

Downstairs at the end of the hall, he rapped on Alexis's room door and waited. After a few moments, the door swung open a foot and Alexis stood there in a robe watching him.

"Mr. Morgan, please come in."

She stepped back and he walked inside and she closed the door. He watched but she didn't lock it. Good.

"Mr. Morgan, please sit in your usual chair and I'll stand here beside the window at a safe distance." She waited as he sat down, then continued.

"Now, Mr. Morgan is it true what I hear around town about the tunnel, and what happened to Julio?" He could see that she had cried a little but there were no serious tear stains.

"I'm not sure what you heard." He followed that by giving her a detailed account of the chase, the fight, the ambush, and then the confrontation in the end of Level Two's main tunnel.

"So it's true that Julio did go into the burial cave and that he was hunting treasure that might be left there with the Indian chiefs?"

"Yes, he said they were buried with gold. Fact is, Indians had no use for gold. Hated it because it was so soft. They called it squaw clay."

"He did fire the shotgun at you inside the burial cave?"

"Yes. I was lucky to duck below the hole in the wall."

He told her again how the shot had buried Julio up to his chest with just one hand out. Then how the sound of their voices might have triggered the rest of the fall that covered him with eight to ten feet of dirt and rocks.

"There was nothing I could do to save him by then. If I had been able to dig down to him, he would have suffocated long before I got there."

She nodded, sniffing a little, then wiping her eyes and looking away. "This is going to take a little time to get used to. I thought I loved him, but at last I understood what he was doing. It hurts. He was using me to get what he wanted. He didn't love me a bit. I know that now."

"So what will you do?"

"Oh, I plan on going back to San Francisco, helping my grandmother all I can. I want to learn as much about her businesses and affairs as I can so I can take over and help her run them. When she at last does die, I'll be able to carry on the way she has. I have tremendous love and respect for my grandmother.

"This unfortunate episode with Julio has helped me to grow up and to realize that life isn't always what we want it to be."

Morgan nodded. "I'm relieved to hear about that."

She laughed. "Besides, if I go back to Grandmother you'll earn a higher fee, right?"

"That could be the case. Would that bother you?"

"Not at all. You're just doing your job, what she hired you to do. Besides, now I realize that it means a great deal to me just to be rid of Julio. I don't see now how I could have been that star struck, that blinded by a few kisses."

Morgan chuckled. "Don't worry about that, young lady. That problem is one most of us just never learn to deal with."

She grinned and looked at him slyly. "Do you remember when I kissed you the other night?"

"Of course. How could I forget?"

She stood and walked up to him standing so close that her breasts almost touched his chest. Her eyes stared hard at him.

"Mr. Morgan, did you enjoy those kisses?"

"Tremendously."

"Good." She leaned against him and stretched up to find his lips with hers. She pressed hard on him from her lips all the way down to her hips and the kiss tingled his mouth and made him want to open it.

When she eased away from him she caught his hand and pulled him toward the bed. She sat down on it and urged him to sit beside her. He looked at her but didn't move.

"Wasn't this in your duties outlined for you by Grandmother? She didn't say that you could kiss me?"

"No such instructions," Morgan said. He took a deep breath. What in hell was he supposed to do now? He was damned either way.

She pulled hard on his arm and he resisted a moment, then gradually sat down beside her. She moved so her leg touched his all the way down.

"Now, that's better. Am I so unattractive, Mr. Morgan?"

"No, you're beautiful, slender and shapely, and so young and fresh it makes me yearn that I had lived ten fewer years."

Alexis beamed. Her face held a beautiful smile, eyes sparkling, pink lips parted, white teeth gleaming.

She waited a moment; then a slight frown dented her smile. "Mr. Morgan, do I have to ask you to kiss me?"

He shook his head, bent and kissed her lips lightly. His lips barely touched hers and she clung to the embrace as lightning raced between their tingling lips. When he pulled back she sighed and leaned in against him.

"Now, Mr. Morgan, there was a beautiful kiss. So tender! I'm amazed and delighted. We can trade. Now this time I get to kiss you."

She leaned toward him, kissed him, then put her hands around his neck and pulled him toward her. As she did she leaned over backward until she lay on the bed and had pulled him with her until he covered half of her young body, his mouth still on hers.

Slowly she opened her lips. Her tongue darted through and hit his lips and she licked them a moment before they opened.

She gave a little moan of joy as her tongue penetrated his mouth for the first time. She came up for breath a few moments later, her hands still around his neck, holding him tightly against her.

Then she pushed him away a few inches, caught his hand and placed it on one of her breasts. The robe was thin and his hand cupped her nearly bare breast. Alexis's eyes danced as she felt him caress her mound with tenderness.

"Oh, Lee Morgan, you can't imagine how wonderful that makes me feel."

Morgan moved his hand and sat up. He lifted her gently beside him and shushed her when she was about to speak.

"Alexis, you know where this is leading?"

"I know. I'm not a virgin. I've made love before, Mr. Morgan and I want to again, right now, right this second with you."

His brow furrowed and she reached up and smoothed out the wrinkles.

"No, Morgan. Don't tell me no. I've been in love with you from that very first time I saw you out at the house. I've dreamed of this moment. Don't take it away from me."

Morgan caught her hand when it reached for his thigh.

"Little lady, let me get a few things straight. I have two more days here waiting for a reply from a wire I send in the morning by stage to Sacramento. Then maybe another day to work out the details. Then I'll be going back to Sacramento to report what's happened to your grandmother."

"Fine, I'll go with you."

"In San Francisco you'll stay with your grandmother, help her, take care of her?"

"Naturally. I want to learn everything that she knows, and I don't have many years. No one knows how many."

Morgan sighed. "You're so damn young."

She punched him in the arm and laughed. "And

you're so damn old." Slowly she undid the fastener
of the robe and slipped it off her shoulders. She let
it come down slowly over her chest; then it edged
downward to show the curve of her breasts.

"Kiss me, Morgan," Alexis said.

Morgan did. Then his lips moved down to the
robe still covering her breasts. Slowly he pushed
the robe lower with his mouth and kissed his
way down until the robe came forward over her
mounds.

A moment later it fell to her waist and Morgan
kissed both breasts, then licked her throbbing nipples and bit each one tenderly.

She lifted his head and kissed his lips, then pulled
him over on the bed again.

She put both his hands on her breasts, then kissed
his lips and came away.

"Mr. Morgan, tonight I want you to show me ten
different ways to make love."

Morgan grinned staring down at the beautiful,
sexy young woman and sighed. "Ten? Hey, I'm
not sixteen anymore. Let's say we'll make a try
for eight."

Alexis kicked away the robe until she was bare
to her toes and slowly spread her legs showing the
thatch of raven hair at her crotch.

Morgan sighed. "Hell, we'll try for nine."

It turned out to be seven.

The next morning Morgan sent his wire on the
stage to Sacramento, then toured the mine with
Bullitt and four other men. Bullitt kept a pad of
paper on a flat board and wrote down what needed
to be done on every level and drift and at each ore
producing face.

By noon they were in the mine office building.
Old Yancy had the keys to the two buildings. The
landslide had damaged only part of one end of

the building. Bullitt put two men to work with a horse and a scraper to remove the dirt and rocks so repairs could be made.

Inside they checked the books and the work force. About a third of the men had found jobs in other local mines, Bullitt told him. A few had moved. Bullitt figured he could get a crew together for one shift in a week.

"We have to wait for final authorization and funding from Mrs. Wheeler," Morgan said. "I have no doubt that she'll go along with my recommendation. I'm putting you in charge as temporary mine manager until a new man can be appointed. Then you'll be second in command and work in any areas that you and the manager decide."

Bullitt grinned and shook Morgan's hand. He had to blink back tears and turned to rub them away.

Morgan and Alexis had dinner that night in the hotel dining room. Helen served them. She glared at Morgan a moment, then shrugged. She took their order and left quickly.

That night Morgan added one new position to Alexis's list of positions and then fell asleep so exhausted that not even her youthful charms could awaken him.

The morning stage from Sacramento brought back word from Mrs. Wheeler. It was a telegram a foot long. It authorized Morgan to open the mine and get it running. Named him temporary general manager or gave him authority to appoint one.

Another wire was a moneygram authorizing Morgan to open the company's bank account and wiring $50,000 to the mine account for operating funds.

Morgan stayed three more days. Bullitt had the mine almost ready to start production. They got word that a new General Manager would arrive the next day.

It took Morgan another day to fill the man in on the local situation. He and Bullitt got along well and worked like an old hand team together. Morgan's job was done.

He and Alexis caught the morning stage to Sacramento and a day later walked into Mrs. Wheeler's San Francisco Nob Hill mansion.

After a flurry of female hugs and kisses, Mrs. Wheeler turned to Morgan. "I've had your bank drafts ready for two days, and I figured in your expenses at twenty dollars a day."

She handed them to him and Morgan pushed them into the inside pocket of his jacket.

"Mrs. Wheeler, I thank you and I predict that this young lady will surprise you in a year or so. She tells me that she wants to learn all she can about your business so she can help you run things."

Mrs. Wheeler brushed a tear from her eyes. "Glory be, my prayers are answered." She hugged her granddaughter. "Morgan, I knew you could do it. Don't see how your pa could have done better."

Morgan thanked her, nodded to a beaming Alexis and went out the door into the hands of the butler who ushered him to the street. Morgan kicked at the sidewalk in delight. Another $10,000 cash in hand. What now? He didn't have the slightest idea. Maybe there would be something interesting in his messages. Lee Buckskin Morgan grinned. He'd figure out something exciting to do. He hurried down the street, anxious now to see what those three weeks of messages might be and who might be asking for help. Morgan laughed softly. It was a great life. He wouldn't have it any other way.